CONFIDENCE JOHN

CONFIDENCE JOHN

HARMONY REED

STERLING & STONE

Chapter One

A REFLECTION on the well floor told her everything. Three points of light. Two were like the staring eyes of a dead man looking up at the last drop of sun he'd ever see. The third was a sparkling star.

Emily paused with the ladle at her lips. A cloud sailed its shadow across her shoulder, and the well went dark. Still, she hesitated.

Footsteps crunched in the sandy courtyard behind her. "I wouldn't drink that, young sir."

Emily tipped her head to thank the man soaking in the swampy depths with a click of her tongue, a wink and a smile.

She let the ladle drop to clatter against the course stone. Twine looped into the handle creaked as it swung.

She straightened the ruffles at her wrists as she turned and lifted her chin to stare down her nose at the approaching figure.

Sniffed. Cleared her throat. Pitched her accent to British. "And why ever not?"

The church looked like it grew out of the surrounding

trees. Cheesecloth shades fluttered over new tobacco plants.

The priest held his cassock close with one hand. Raised the other in greeting. His face was red and puffy in the blazing heat. Emily found it curious that he wore no hat against the pounding sun.

He dropped his hand when she didn't return his wave, but the grin went nowhere. "We believe some young Creek raiders may have dropped a deer in the well."

Emily widened her eyes as she pulled her beaver gaucho hat off and slapped the dust on her thigh. "This close to Georgia?"

The priest spread his hands. "The magistrate is enlisting a host of Spaniards laying over for a letter from Andrew Jackson. I fear the governor has more pressing business, however."

The priest wore his robes like a costume, in wrinkles and rumples that didn't fall right. Emily herself could understand. She was dressed as a young man looking for his way in the world.

A young man of means, and worldly. Cotton vest and jacket from England. Silk tie and handkerchief from India. Soft leather riding boots. Her pistols and saber were made by French masters, her saddle hand-tooled by Jans Brigham himself.

But unlike the priest's welcome, hers was without flaw. She presented as a New England dandy. *His* pretense as a southern priest was offensive.

The accent was not Florida. Not Spanish or French. A slight lilt suggested Ireland by way of the Pennsylvania railroad gandy dancers working their way down the coast.

His sunburned nose and pale eyes helped confirm it.

Emily donned her hat with a flourish. "Not aught to drink in the meantime, Father?"

The priest shrugged again. "I have fresh coffee. Strong and sweet. Some goat's milk with a day or two left on it."

Emily nodded and extended her hand. "I have full skins still. Warm and salty, but I had a taste for something cool. Emmett Bisset, at your service."

The priest took her hand in a crushing grip. She had learned long ago to wrestle in greeting. Give as good as she got.

The priest's grin faltered. A flash of uncertainty, but he regained his aplomb in an instant. "A pleasure, young sir. Chase Emmanuel."

Emily pulled her hand back and slid her fingers into her vest pocket. "And have you caught them, Father?"

His eyes narrowed in confusion, then widened in understanding. "Ah, 'tis not my calling of late, my son. To chase the sinners toward salvation. Nay, I save souls the Lord *sends* me."

Emily grunted laughter. "Even if they're not Catholic?"

Chase threw his head back in laughter. His watery eyes crinkled at the corners. "Down here? *Everyone* is Catholic."

He pointed at Emily's rig sitting in the sand at her feet — saddle and bags, toilette and bedroll. "Can I help you carry your things to where you want?"

Emily tipped her head toward the church. "Where I want is right there, Father. I would accept your help, as I'm spent from days inside a jouncing carriage. And despite the heat, I would also accept the offer of coffee, if offer it truly was."

"A young soul seeking out one of my humble vocation? I would be honored."

Emily stooped for the saddle. Tipped her head toward the bags. "The honor is mine, Father. I'm most grateful."

She saw his eyes crawl over the plain scabbard and the wax seal on the veneered box that carried her guns.

His brow furrowed with worry as he stood with his burden.

She stepped aside to wait for his lead and followed him over cobbles hidden by unswept sand. Through the front doors, and the church was still, save for rustling sheers over the side windows. A breeze helped cool the thin sweat on her cheeks and upper lip.

Chase threw his hip to the side, avoiding a collision with the chair holding the door open. "This way, my son. My chamber has a wide window that faces the garden."

No bowl of blessed water. No burning candles.

Emily hitched the saddle up over the top of the girdle flattening her chest and laid her wrist against the knife handle hidden by her vest.

Like a kitten burrowing for the teat. It was a need fulfilled. Comfort.

Chase passed through a narrow door leading into the priest's seating chamber. She waited for him to clear it, and he set her bags on a worn bench beside a wicker desk.

He stood straight with a groaning stretch, and the hem lifted from his boots.

More curious than the absence of a hat in the Florida blaze, was a priest with spurs. He'd stuffed tufts of dirty linen through to keep them silent.

Emily settled the saddle on the floor and turned to Chase with a bow of thanks. "I know water slakes a man's thirst, Father, but is there something else that might nourish your spirit?"

Chase laid his finger along the side of his nose. "Spirit for spirit, my son? If you have it to offer?"

"I do indeed."

"Then, I accept."

"Splendid." Emily clapped her hands and grinned. "We shall both pour, then."

Chase turned with a nod, and she suspected his smile was finally genuine.

He ambled to a small iron stove and turned a coal with a pair of blackened tongs. Then he took two clay mugs from a shelf and poured thick coffee from a dented tin carafe.

Emily met him with a flask full of brandy. When she offered him the first dollop, and Chase rolled his eyes in pleasure at the aroma alone.

He poured a healthy splash, then looked up with a mischievous smile that brought a chuckle through her nose. She imitated his pour, and before capping the flask, they clinked their mugs in a moment of companionship she was sure was a surprise for them both.

The brandy did little to tame the coffee's bitterness, but managed to calm her fingers.

Chase smacked his lips, closing his eyes in appreciation. "There is little else in the world that proves God's love to me."

He pointed to the empty chair in front of the desk. "Please, sit. Be my guest."

Emily set her mug on the stained doily next to a Bible with a cracked spine, capped the flask, and sat with a nod of gratitude. The chair creaked like sailing ropes. She took the mug back and watched Chase sit behind the desk. He barely fit. It had been meant for a much smaller man.

She looked down over the rim of her mug as she took another sip. The rug was askew.

Moved from its original location. The section of the floor not faded from the sun was still rich with color, in the shape of the rug's border.

Moved to reveal or to hide?

She pulled her hat from her head. Rested it on her

knee. Smoothed her hair down into the style held by the French beeswax.

"What are your thoughts, Father?"

"On what, my son?"

Emily smiled over her cup. "Not to put too fine a point on it, but on *me*?"

Chase took a long sip before setting the cup on his desk, ignoring the doily next to the blotter. "Not many come through here with a full kit. I suspect the livery men turned you away empty handed, as there are no horses for sale this close to the border."

"That is correct."

Chase acknowledged her words with a smug smile. "And I can't help wondering if your destination was not this town, but this church."

"Correct again."

"The caretaker before me spoke about strangers with strange requests. I have yet to encounter any, but then you have made none."

"How long have you been here, Father?"

He sat back in surprise, lifting his eyes as if to think. "Oh, I have been at this for a very long time."

Emily had seen enough. She drank the last of the coffee, chewed on the grounds before putting the mug down. "I will come to it, then. I am here for a box."

Chase leaned forward and steepled his fingers. "A box, my son?"

"Well, the *contents* of a box."

Chase nodded. His black sleeves slid down his arms. The white linen underneath was pitted with burn holes. Sparks from a blacksmith's fire, maybe. Or the spitting coal of a steam engine.

"The caretaker before me mentioned that very thing. And he told me there would be … a token. Something shown as proof the bearer was ... qualified to view the contents of that box."

"And did the previous caretaker say what that token was to be?"

Chase narrowed his eyes and leaned back. "He did not. He only said it would be one half of a heart."

"And the heart?"

"One belonging to a great man. A war hero. A *scoundrel*. The heart of Confidence John."

Emily held his gaze. Reached into her watch pocket. The brass was cold under her fingers. "There was a baby born here. To a woman suffering a cruel addiction. The priest at the time, perhaps the very caretaker of whom you spoke, took her and the baby into the bosom of the church, and he attempted to cure the woman, but alas ..."

Chase sat with his mouth open, staring at her lips as she told her tale.

She pressed the release, and the watch sprang open, but there were no gears inside. No glass. No time at all.

Only history.

She looked up at the ceiling, momentarily breaking his gaze. "The woman left, and the father decided not to follow. He was quit of her, you see. Of her and her lies. The lies into which she raised an innocent."

There was half a coin inside the case. A copper challenge coin from the war against the British. She lifted it out and set it on the desk. It landed with an empty clink.

"The father ignored them both, until one day ... for reasons untold, he sought them out. Many years passed before he found that child — confused by life, and angry. He gave the child that coin. Mated it with the other half he wore on a chain, and he told the child it was the other half of his heart. He also said the child was the other half of his soul, but the child did not believe that."

Emily slid the coin across the desk. Chase picked it up like the treasure it was.

"Decades later, the child learned the man did a strange thing. He left a treasure for that child to find. In *this* church." She reached into the watch pocket again, and she pulled out an iron key. "Opened with this."

Chase stared at the key like he had witnessed a great magic trick, and he shook his head. "You are not the child, yes?"

"Does it matter? I have the coin and the key."

"Where did you get them?"

She remembered the look on Gaston Grey's face when she ran him through. Beaten by a woman. The shame so plain in his eyes as he drew his last breath.

He may have had the key, but only she and her mother knew where the church was. Gaston had thought to use Emily. Force himself into her bed at knifepoint. Take her body by force. Dig the location of the church from her tortured brain.

Disgusting man. He'd died better than he deserved. She resisted the shudder that tightened her belly muscles at the memory of his hands on her skin.

She shrugged. "It matters not the where or the how."

He sat straight as if waking up. "Perhaps not."

He slid the coin back with a nod. Pushed his chair back and bent down.

The coin went back into the watch case. The case back into the pocket.

She smiled when he flipped the edge of the rug back and lifted a chair leg to use the weight to hold the flap down. He'd been looking already.

He grunted and heaved a small iron chest out of a dusty hole in the floor. His red face darkened into scarlet, and he leaned back to get the bottom clear of the desk, dropping the chest with a groaning sigh of relief.

The desk bowed in the center, popping and snapping in protest, but it held.

Chase gasped in triumph and stepped back to wait with his hands on his hips.

Emily felt a cold knot in her chest. Not a thrill, but dread.

Chase shuffled around the side of the desk as she slotted the key. It turned as if the lock had been recently oiled, with only a whisper of resistance.

The opening lid sounded like a saber drawn from its scabbard.

The eyes at the bottom of the well had been a warning. The third glint in the depths was the cross around the dead priest's neck. The previous caretaker had been pushed to his death, and the current resident now stood behind her holding her own saber over his head.

The knife handle was in her hand — drawn and positioned as she spun away from his swing.

The curved blade of her saber bit into the desk with the sound of a mallet to the wedge. Chase's eyes bulged with a killing fever, but it was her knife that fulfilled his desire for death.

She struck from her crouch like a hot geyser erupting from the earth, thrusting with the knife. It slid between his ribs as if the man were made of cheese.

The impact sent bright pain through her joints as it lifted the false priest from his feet.

Bitter coffee on his breath washed across her face, and they fell back with the same scream rising in terrible harmony.

She rode him to the floor, their bodies crashing down

to the worn planks. She rose to settle her weight on the blade, and his ribs creaked under her hand.

His clawed fingers scraped at her forearms. Then he collapsed flat, and his gaze focused on her face. He stilled when he made it to her eyes.

The blade was in his heart.

His mouth pleaded without sound. He licked his lips and shook his head. Took a shallow breath. "You are not the son of Confidence John."

She tightened her grip. "Of course not. I could never have been such."

His smug smile returned, but it withered when she freed the knife with a jerk. His life pulsed over her knuckles.

She rested the edge against his throat. "For I'm his *daughter*."

She drew it across his neck in a brutal slash, and his smile relaxed as his mouth filled with blood.

Chapter Two

Simone kneaded the fabric of her silk apron. She wore the blue dress with the white lacing, to the ankle so that she could flash the tops of her dyed leather slippers.

Far too old for such behavior, but she was still toothsome, and Jefferson Atwell took pleasure in seeing her that way. In fact, many men directed their eyes to her form, both dashed and lingering gazes darting down to linger on her powdered cleavage. But only Jefferson truly knew her. Only he could love her with the heat of a fire.

How she wished she could return that love.

Claudia and her daughter, Yuliana, stood by the pantry door in identical postures of contrition.

The two Cuban women were both small. Coppery brown, as if gold flowed beneath their tanned skin. They were more like sisters.

Simone thought of her own Emily, gone for so long. Did they still look like each other?

Would people guess they were mother and daughter?

Her thoughts had distracted her. *Selfish* thoughts, no less. Painful memories were for another time.

Like when she and Jefferson were in each other's arms in the sweltering dark, the flicker of a bare candle flame glistening off the skin of his powerful shoulders.

She shook her head and forced a smile. Selfish distractions.

Simone addressed the woman on the left. "*Que es, Claudia? No temas. Estará bien* … please."

Both women looked up, their eyes shining with unshed tears and foreheads wrinkled with worry. Claudia pressed a stained handkerchief to her forehead. "*Viene un bebe.*"

Simone dug her fingers into her apron and stepped back. "A baby coming …" She turned to Yuliana. "You're pregnant?"

The young woman drew back. Her puzzled eyes narrowed, then widened before crinkling with her smile. "No, Miss Simone. My *mother* is pregnant. Not me."

Simone leaned forward and took her hands. Said she was happy for her. "*Estoy tan feliz por ti.*"

Simone dabbed the corners of her eyes with her thumb. Queen Victoria may have thought eyeliner and rouge were for prostitutes, but *she* didn't have to worry about declining beauty. She was the bloody queen. Who would dare tell her she was looking a little pale today?

Claudia's words were a tumble of sound, and tears of gratitude filled her eyes. Simone pulled her into an embrace. "Have you told Joshua?"

Claudia nodded against her, and Yuliana chuckled. "My father ran from the house without his shirt, stomping and cursing. It was frightful."

Joshua Hines was an escaped slave, offered asylum in Florida by the Spanish government in exchange for his conversion to Catholicism. But with the laws being rewritten daily and the promise of statehood in the balance, Florida was as deadly as it had ever been. Even when compared to the hardships Joshua had endured while fighting his way through the South — wars between France and America, Spain and America, Britain and America, and now the biggest battle of them all, inside America herself.

He'd made it to her finishing school here in St. Augustine, and she'd financed his new life. Hid him from those who had chased him across the border and watched him fall for a Cuban woman in her employ.

Scars from the whip twisted the skin on his back. To go outside without his shirt — he must have been lost in his emotions indeed.

He often hid on his boat, a small schooner he sailed down to the waters off *Cayo Hueso,* where he dragged his iron rake for sponges. The holds beneath were often filled with runaway slaves heading for Spain by way of Cuba. Then, tobacco and rum on the return trip.

What he didn't smoke and drink, he turned over to her, and Jefferson and Buford carried it north to sell in Boston.

The money helped keep her underground railroad in desperately needed funds. But her main source of income came via the monthly steamer from *El Halconito*. Confidence John knew the struggle of financing an illegal business. She just wished it was him stepping from the gangway instead of his porter.

That was unfair to Jefferson, but she couldn't deny the hold Confidence John still had on her heart.

"I'm sure he's just worried for you," she said to Claudia. "He loves you, doesn't he?"

Yuliana translated, and like Simone, Claudia maintained her attention on the speaker instead of the interpreter. She shook her head, and her words were a rush of emotion.

"No, Miss Simone. He is afraid that you will not let her

work. That you will send her away, and our family will break."

Simone gasped, lacing her hands over her heart. "That is absurd."

Yuliana threw her hands up in frustration. "That's what I told him. *Both* of them."

The bell over the front door rang. Footsteps on the polished floorboards, and a wash of noise from outside. Horseshoes on cobbles. Sellers crying from the boardwalk. Children laughing like birdsong.

Simone lowered herself until she was eye to eye with Claudia and squeezed her shoulders for emphasis. "You will always be welcome here."

Yuliana parroted her in Spanish, and Claudia's tears flowed anew.

"You have the run of my business," Simone continued. "You own all of my secrets, and your *tostones* are divine."

This should never have been an issue. But she was a white lady. *La dama blanca.* And Claudia was a servant in a land that once belonged to her people.

Times changed, but people never seemed to.

She left them both laughing through their tears, moving from the kitchen into the reception parlor that served as the storefront of *Miss Simone's School for the Socially Displaced*.

On the surface, it was a place of rehabilitation for freed slaves, outcast Indians, and those separated from society for misbehavior — divorce, released prisoners, and others that had lost their honor. But underneath, it served as a secret route for the transport of individuals on the run from the persecution of slavery.

A far more noble cause that she'd adopted *after* she'd found a way out of her own dishonor.

She scrubbed her hands on the bottom of her apron

and patted her hair down and smoothed her skirts. She had her suspicions about who had come to call, and she wasn't disappointed.

Well … not much.

Father Alonso Sebastian stood with his hands behind his back. His wide-brimmed hat rested on his shoulder, hanging from the raw cord pulled taut across his throat.

He grinned with yellow teeth stained by rum and cigar smoke. His thin mustache looked like it had been drawn on with coal.

A black man stood like a shadow behind him, staring at the floor and wringing a felt hat in his gnarled hands. His low voice rumbled a nervous tune as he muttered something under his breath.

Alonso spread his arms. "Miss Simone. So lovely to see you."

His words hissed through his accent, broad and full, like a stage actor's impression of Spain.

She returned his grin with a polite smile and held her arms out to receive his chaste embrace. "Father Alonso, my home has been empty without your presence."

He pulled away to look up at her with reproach. "Oh, but lady. It is the presence of the Lord that should be ever on your mind."

She stepped back and touched her hand over her heart, playing her own role in the performance he required. "With my Baptist upbringing, I can do no less but think of Him, ever watchful."

"Miss Simone, you are too kind."

"I think not, Father, but I do try. How can I be of service today?"

He gave his head an emphatic shake. "No, no. It is I who must be of service."

"But you do so much, already."

She loathed this requirement. The exchange of empty words. Alonso thought it was a clever way to hide their deeds from those who would persecute them.

Instead, it made him a fool. Acting like he kept a secret made it a surety that a secret would be seen. But so far, it had cost her nothing to play along. Who was she to the authorities, but a widow using her inheritance to improve her world? Misguided and flighty. A role she played with pleasure.

But there were times …

The doorway into the "classroom" filled with the formidable shape of Jefferson Atwell. A man too young to have seen so much of war, his body bore the scars that only she could see. Tall and hard. Broad shoulders and narrow waist. He looked like the memory of a man she couldn't let go. A fitting stand-in for Confidence John.

Theirs was a romance of youthful enthusiasm, though they were fifteen years apart. He knew her heart was in the past, but still, he loved her.

He was followed by Buford. A massive man of gravity, his skin dark like wet leather, cracked and lined like old boots. Though never chased through the swamps on his way to freedom, he'd claimed sanctuary of the church. As a Catholic convert trading his faith for asylum, his status was now in question. With the Florida territory changing hands again, there was no official of any government willing to stand against the slave owners sending marauding posses across the border.

Yet he stayed with her — a humble man of intense loyalty. She would trust him with the most precious thing on earth.

Hatken was the third man to enter the front room. *The White One*. A Seminole warrior and outcast, shunned for the streaks of white in his skin and hair. Nearly the entire left side of his face was absent of color, his left hand pale as a maggot's belly.

His people knew of him. Even dealt with him in trade and information. But they kept him apart, even as they were driven from their lands.

Time and again.

He'd fought for his people in the French and Indian Wars. But they cast him out still, and he'd taken up with a group of travelers moving south along the coast to St. Augustine, where he met Miss Simone. He thought her a wise woman. A *great* woman.

Like Jefferson, he was young. And just as she thought she was unworthy of one man's love, she felt unworthy of the other's respect.

Alonso blinked in surprise. His gaze darted to the doorway, running over the approaching men. An audience come late to the performance.

His brow furrowed, shoulders drooping like a flower longing for water. She waited for him to regain his thoughts as the men assumed their positions along the wall.

"Though I risk offending you, that is nonsense. We are both servants of God. And to that end, I must keep my place at His side assured."

He stepped aside while extending his arm to point at the man behind him. "This is Julius. He has requested a place in my church, but as you know, we are in trying times, Miss Simone. Trying times, indeed."

Simone smiled and stepped forward, with her hand out in greeting. Julius looked at it with widened eyes. His mouth fell open, and his lower lip shook with fear. She moved with care as she bent to take his hand in hers. "You are welcome here, Julius."

He looked up from her hand in amazement. His fear tore at her heart.

Alonso pushed between them, smiling in satisfied triumph. "As I explained to him, now I have proven."

She wished he had found her first. It would have saved him the fear — and her the money.

She stepped back and tipped her head toward the waiting men. Julius followed her gaze with fear slowing his head as he turned. "This is Buford."

He came forward with a warm smile, and Julius' mouth twitched in response. Like he was forcing it to be still.

She moved around Alonso to lay her hand on Buford's shoulder. "He will take you to the kitchen. Please tell him your story, and fear not for the day."

She knew Alonso had kept the man well-hidden. Just not well-fed. The priest was a miser when it came to the comfort of others.

As Buford took the hesitant man in with an arm across his shoulders, Simone turned back to the priest. He watched the men leave as if witnessing the birth of a child.

She forced her sneer into a beaming grin. "It is generous of you to shield those without defense, Father."

"Especially in such days as these," he replied. "When Spain's protection flees like the French and British before them."

She clutched her hands together. Her act wasn't yet complete. "There must be some way to repay your parish for the sacrifice."

He held his hands up in protest, as he always did. "No, Lady. I could not, for I am on the path God has set me."

Simone reached into her apron pocket and removed a leather pouch. It was heavy with gold.

Despite his protests, Father Sebastian's hand opened to receive the pouch. She bowed as she let the drawstring slide from her fingers. "It is but a donation to aid those in need, Father. Mete it out as you see fit."

The pouch disappeared. "Bless you, my child. *Stultus sapit, cum tacet.*"

A fool is wise when silent. She was sure about the *fool* part, but she kept her own silence.

She took his hands in hers, barely keeping the disgust from her face. His palms were clammy. Like moist bread. "The least I can do for delivering to me one in such need. Will I see you in the plaza this evening?"

The sudden change brought him up short. There were usually several minutes of preening, an extended farce to make him feel like a man of mystery. But her stomach recoiled at the thought of spending any more time in his presence than necessary.

He gave her an uncertain nod. "Yes, of course. The penitents need guidance."

"Lovely, Father."

She turned him toward the door with a gentle push on his shoulder. His body moved under her hand, and he was walking under the jangling bell before he could even protest.

She pulled the door closed and turned back inside. A brief glimpse of his confused disappointment brought an unlikely giggle to her throat. "Lord, give me patience."

Hatken pushed off the wall, hooking his thumb at the glass windows facing the street as he moved toward the kitchen. "That man is a donkey's ass."

Jefferson offered his arm to her before shaking his head at Hatken's back. "That's calling him an ass twice, ain't it?"

"That's right," Hatken said. "Because he's a double."

Simone thought the Indian was being far too kind.

Chapter Three

Emily had killed a man for an iron chest full of letters and a leather-bound journal so heavily oiled, the pages had turned the color of churned earth. The journal, she couldn't read. The letters, she wouldn't.

She paid extra to be alone inside a coach that smelled like stale air and bile, despite the wide thrown shutters. Three days spent bouncing and sweating, and not once did she ogle her treasure.

There was no blood on her jacket, but her shirt cuffs were soaked through. She passed the time by removing the sleeves, stitch by stitch, with the knife she'd dragged across the imposter's throat.

She tossed the fabric out the window to flutter into tall grass at the trail's edge. Considered throwing herself out as well.

At least with the alligators, she wouldn't have to pretend.

Acting like a man made achieving her dreams as easy as waking, but living as a woman turned life into a trial.

She worked harder than most men she'd ever met. And was a better man than many.

Her illusion was complete. Her body honed into a shape that let her pass the deep scrutiny she barely encountered anymore. Neck and shoulders. Thickened and broadened through labor.

Body fat burned off in combat.

Years behind the saber facing Louis Cheval, a *sabreur* of divine grace and expertise. She had thought to get close to him. Seduce him. Become his apprentice … and perhaps more. But his obsession with her was a tragedy, for he thought her a man in truth.

Their shared disappointment brought them as close to lovers as they could ever be.

He turned her into the man he wished she was. Dress and manners. Thought and deed. But the torture of knowing she would never be real drove him to destruction. *La merveille.*

She'd been his second in a duel against Marcus de Galle, all parties involved drunk on rum. Pistols were chosen, and though she cautioned him, Louis agreed to the terms.

He was far better with steel than lead.

His shot hit Marcus in the thigh, a bloody wound that invited a month of limping.

The return shot put a ball in his belly, and the only man she'd ever loved died screaming in her arms after three days of agony and fever.

"Tu n'as jamais été à moi."

His dying whisper had been correct. She'd never belonged to him. But she never belonged to herself, either.

No, Emily was a slave to what should have been. And not just the lost life of one little girl, but the lives of all girls mistreated by the ones who were supposed to love and protect them.

Mothers, like Simone Bisset. Selling every beautiful thing for the comfort of poppy. Her body. Her soul. Even her daughter.

Fathers, like Confidence John. A liar and a cheat. Or as Chase called him — a scoundrel.

And a daughter … so dramatic. She sighed at the ceiling.

It wasn't like Emily to lament. Perhaps it was the drink making her so. She smiled into her glass. A thick port the likes of which a gentleman would share with his comrades.

But she was alone, and the rum from the coach had since faded from memory.

This rotten settlement rising out of a festering bog was the only stop on her journey to the Atlantic coast — a Seminole village growing into a town on the way to somewhere else. From there to the sea, where she would hire a boat to take her south, to the island where her father lived. To the big game, the Gran Behike Tournament. Confidence John filled his den with the world's greatest card players. A fortune to enter, and the winner could buy the kingdom of his choice. Or hers.

But Emily wasn't going there to win, though she was invited by Confidence John himself, gaining his attention at the Baccarat tables in France.

Eight months of travel and preparation, and she was still short the entrance fee. She'd thought the church in Quincy would provide the remainder, but it was empty of everything but mystery.

Strange that Confidence John would seek out his lost daughter in the same year he announced the last tournament he would ever host. He wanted to make amends? He was dying?

She fingered the knife handle under her vest. She would assure him of both.

A rowdy in a beaver skin jacket lifted his glass of warm beer for what felt like the twelfth time. A man more interested in the shape of his mustache than the odor of that ridiculous coat. The air barely moved inside the parlor, but he was buttoned up tight.

He eyed her when she first walked in. Sucked his teeth and tipped his hat. Smiled with only half his mouth.

She hadn't bothered with a room, just a bath rental and a changing room key. When she came out to find a table, he was staring at her still.

She took her seat, with an uncorked bottle and a dirty glass. Beaver's gaze flickered to the bar, and a tall man in long black tails, tight black trousers, and polished boots stepped back. He strolled across the stained carpet to stand at her shoulder.

His bore the slight lisp of a Spanish aristocrat. "It is best to be direct, don't you think?"

She watched his reflection in the dark port bottle. Laid her arm over her chest to feel the shape of the knives in her vest. She sniffed as she filled her glass with her other hand.

His voice became a whisper, barely heard above the parlor's din. "Then as I have often counseled, so shall I be. Boy or girl?"

The sweat in the hollow of her back chilled. An icy breath that rose up to blow across her shoulder blades and the nape of her neck. She ground her teeth against the shiver that threatened to bounce her from her seat.

How had he known?

She had long thought her presentation to be perfect. From the turmeric dye on her face to the sack of rice tied behind the buttons of her trousers. Masculine stubble and manly bulge. There was never a soul to suspect, until now.

Her hand crept into the slit concealed by the lacing on her collar. She could take his eyes with a single swing. Be across the room before the echo of his scream returned to him.

A dispute between gentlemen.

The man leaned forward on the prop of his ornate cane. "It is also *polite* to ask, is it not?"

Emily nearly gasped in relief when understanding settled over her heart. She smiled and raised her glass in a silent toast. "*Caballero*, I prefer women."

He stamped the floor with the silver point. "Ah, that is a shame. You have the cut of one that might have a libertine spirit."

Her tailors had all been French, and she was of an age to have associated with the rise of the Sadists in Paris. The man was not to blame for his assumption. "No sir, I cannot but note my assignment with the cavalry abroad. Released by the cessation of offense betwixt two countries."

The man's teeth flashed in the bottle's reflection. "And you have chosen for your return to be this place? I commend your tolerance." He bowed over his cane, covering his heart with a silken hand. "*Señor Remu de la Vega.* If you change your mind. Please, call on me. I will be your servant, sir."

She caught the ugly man in the beaver coat watching, but his gaze was on the Spaniard moving from behind her. Remu de la Vega shook his head upon passing, and his oiled curls scattered the light streaming through the open doors. His aroma was sandalwood and sweat.

Not unpleasant.

Beaver nodded in understanding. Turned away with a

cock of his head. Directed de la Vega to the side entrance leading to the dining room.

There were children there. Along the wall.

Having paused for a polite request to bed her, he was now on his way to seek out a different form of entertainment.

But that had been his intent all along, and Emily had misunderstood his question twice.

She dried the rim of her glass. Filled it again, and sat back to wait with the knife in her other hand. She would finish the bottle. Then surprise the Spaniard with pleasure more sadistic than he could imagine.

Perhaps the child she saved would rescue another in turn.

If only somebody had done for her — but then Emily thought she was doing just fine and dandy. So long as there was drink.

Another glass empty, and she watched Beaver and de la Vega exit the parlor.

Men were predators. Fragile with suppressed emotion and fear, but predators nonetheless. She had become one herself. After believing yet another lie at the hands of those who knew no better.

Another man had once pulled her from the dark under the back stairs of her mother's house. The clump of the Spaniard's boots on the creaking treads had sounded just like the opium callers. Men in need of her mother, coming with the payment of a drug's escape.

That long ago day, she'd cowered away from the rough hands she'd expected, and instead looked up into a face much like hers. Hawkish and angular. Eyes like polished steel. And lips curving up in an unexpected smile.

Her father. Confidence John.

She had been taught to hate him, but his voice sounded like warm wool. He smelled like leather and cigar smoke.

She looked at her own hands holding the empty port glass. Crisscrossed with scars. Palms covered in calluses from a hundred duels. Hands no lover wanted in a caress.

She snorted laughter as she poured.

His words had been apologies and promises. It felt like a reunion, though they had never met before. And when he took Simone into his arms, Mother and Father together for the first time in Emily's short life, she knew the world had changed.

Simone had been a stinking wreck of sweat and regret, horrified at the love he still claimed for her. She'd sent a terrified glance at Emily over the tall man's shoulder. But Confidence John had appeared so resolute against Simone's fear.

An appearance Emily only achieved after years of trial and error.

That very night, he'd taken her to a tree above the town. So distant in memory it was, she no longer knew its name.

There, he'd showed her the coin. Pressed it into her hand. Promised he would never leave again.

But British soldiers rode through that night, too. The next morning, her father was gone.

Simone had made her fry cakes. Butter and honey — so sweet it seemed to brighten the sun.

For three days, Emily had waited before there was another knock at the door. Simone told her to get under the stairs, and there Emily listened to another man climb into her mother's bedroom.

She'd run off under a dim bit of starlight with nothing but the half coin clutched in her fist.

A hard life for a child.

Beaver and de la Vega emerged with a young boy in tow. Shirtless and beautiful, a Seminole child with exquisite hair like shining crow feathers. His shoulders were straight because he had not yet learned to bow under the weight of shame. Or he was still strong enough to present himself to the buyer as trained.

He followed without protest, and the trio ascended the carpeted stairs.

A hard life indeed.

Emily finished the last swallow of port. Rancid. Spoiled like the touch of lecherous abandon. She stood without hurry and crossed to the bar.

The keeper watched with bored eyes, until she dropped a bag heavy with silver *reales* on the gouged wood. The bag disappeared into the folds of his apron, and he leaned forward. Emily lifted her gaze to the floor above. "The Spanish gentleman and his hideous porter. What room are they in, please?"

The keeper's gaze fell to her waist. Crawled up her body in blatant appraisal. When he looked into her eyes, his knowing smile was a sneer that matched her roiling gut.

Oily and wrong.

Even for someone to *think* such a thing of her, made Emily ill beyond measure.

The keeper's eyebrows rose above his wink. "End of the north hall."

The stairs didn't creak like the ones in her memory. They were soft and silent as she climbed.

Her father's journal was full of code. Indecipherable. But like her deception, the writing looked like … something. Familiar. A foggy memory. Like a woman pretending to be a man.

The letters were plain in language and content. The words of lovers exchanged over distance. But after a slight study of those words, her eyes had lit upon a single word.

Love.

She turned into the hallway atop the stairs, walking in the center of the colorful runner. Turned left at the end. Faced north.

There were clues in the journal. Answers in the letters. Both hidden by the man that wrote them. And only one thing of interest to her.

An address on the coast. Simone Bisset in St. Augustine.

She tapped on the door with the tip of her knife. Scurrying noise inside, like her mother hiding the pipe, her caller covering his body with a dirty sheet. Harsh whispers.

The door swung open, and she uncoiled at the knees. *Balestra* and lunge, then the knife rose to penetrate the underside of Beaver's chin, leaving the blade visible through his garishly stretched lips.

Blood flooded from his nose as he staggered back, limbs darting out like a puppet snatched from the stage by its strings. The door latched as his knees hit the floor.

His bulging eyes rolled up as his body collapsed. He gurgled a final sigh.

Remu de la Vega rose from the bed. Already nude, he held the cane across his body in defense.

His arousal faltered as he jerked the hidden blade free.

The Seminole boy stared from the pillows, looking back over his shoulder with unconcerned eyes. He was empty. Saving him from this thing still made her too late.

For both of them.

De la Vega's footing was a soft mattress full of down. His thrust was awkward and slow.

She came down under his blade, and drove her own into the soft flesh above his pubis.

It bore him down to land seated against the brass head-board. His teeth snapped shut against the hissing wheeze of his breath.

He fought to fill his lungs. Raised his chin to scream his agony at the ceiling.

She drove her knee into his throat. The crunch of cartilage. The ring of his skull against metal.

Emily rolled to the side. Scooped up the boy as she dropped to her feet.

She held him against her, and they watched de la Vega suffocate.

The blade in his bladder bobbed with his slowing heartbeat. Like a second erection.

One that could only cause pain to its owner.

The boy turned away with disinterest — or revulsion — but Emily watched to the very end.

Chapter Four

It took Simone three days to get Julius on Joshua's boat.

There was no urgency. Not as much need for secrecy as in the old days. It used to be exciting and dangerous. Now it was routine.

Like life.

It was this place. A territory caught in the incessant ebb and flow of power. Foreign nations at war with a recently independent United States. A new government with a fresh Congress, in a land without laws save for what a man chose to obey.

And in the balance, the lives of those running away from oppression, slavery, and murder.

A noble cause into which she had thrown herself decades past: rescuing those on the run from evil just as she had been saved from an evil of her own, one that had threatened to obliterate her life. But as was so often the case when God directed a sinner's redemption, the destruction passed her by.

It was her children that had suffered.

On restless mornings, she often walked to the boardwalk to stare out at the crashing waves and the sparkle of the sun as it climbed into the sky. This morning had been the more restless than most.

As she reluctantly walked home, Simone sighed at her reflection in a glass storefront window. Wavy and pocked with bubbles. Like the windows were made of dirty sugar.

The clamor of passing horses snapped her back to the scene in the street. She brought the laced handkerchief to her mouth as she watched the team pull an ornate coach toward the docks. Ladies dressed like her came into view, being escorted to the shops in nervous clusters by sons and cousins outfitted to present a vision of courtly protection. They lifted their hems above the unswept cobbles, dainty toes finding stones untouched by horse dung, pale faces pinched in disgust and concentration.

Showing the rest of the town they had money. Just not *too* much.

Where they gathered together, Simone stood alone. A woman of two reputations. Proper and polite. A war widow. Clueless and flighty.

She was safe on these streets, for the people saved by her *second* reputation would see her come to no harm.

Another coach, pulled by a thundering team of horses, and the little birds with their lace parasols scattered. Simone spread her hand to cover her smile.

The passing coach was stayed with iron strips; its bolted doors had arrow slits instead of windows. The Commander's carriage.

The soldiers were leaving St. Augustine, but militias would remain, appointed by men intent on filling the emptiness left by Spain's receding tide.

The Spanish would remain as a port authority, but once Spain's army followed her navy into the sea, St. Augustine would be without law.

For how long?

Governor Andrew Jackson seemed filled with an insane hate of the Indian man, and some speculated that his aim was the presidency. What better way for him to help secure it than to receive a territory into statehood? Florida would be governed by an authority made powerful with monies earned from a greater government that enforced justice only to those deemed worthy of humanity.

Whites.

Georgia's push into Florida would be swift during this absence of power. Wealthy landowners and their private armies, united in a righteous quest for vengeance and retrieval.

There was still the protection of the church, but anti-Catholic rhetoric was rampant in newspapers, and on the tongues of those emboldened by Spain's departure.

They were in the trough of the tidal wave before it rose up to crash against the shore. Putting Julius on Joshua's boat had been her final task. Everyone she had ever trusted with her secret was now in danger.

She had been a person terrible beyond description for so long, how could she possibly judge others, despite the color of their skin? Sex with strangers to feed an addiction. Banditry and theft. Lives in her trust ruined by her consuming need to suffer. Punishing herself further.

She knew how awful a man could be. How low a woman could bend.

And still, she was told she was better than the Africans and Indians, and only because she was white.

Confidence John had never said such things. He had been a man of fairness. And even though he had introduced her to the life she would eventually fall into, he had not made her choose.

She had done that all on her own.

One of the ladies in the street fell to her knees with a squeak of panic. A young man with a sword on his hip jumped to her rescue, and the driver roared at his team.

The horses reared and screamed. Hooves scraped grooves into the street, sparking off stone with an echoing crack.

The lady birds flocked to their sister, and their protectors shook angry fists at the driver sitting atop the Commander's carriage — the four armored soldiers sitting on the roof.

A dark shape behind her shaded the store window, and instead of her reflection, Simone could see the store's interior.

Mannequins covered in the latest fashion from New Orleans.

Dresses with thin fabrics, high hems, and plunging necklines.

Hats like the plumage of peacocks. Scandalous what modern youth were wearing. The outfits did look cooler than hers, she thought, dabbing at the sheen of sweat on her wrists.

One of the customers shifted from the counter to face the window. Small-waisted, but wide and solid. Short blond hair with a gleaming part. He dressed much like the dandies behind her, but his demeanor was more assured than the children playing at adulthood. He seemed as fashionable as her wares, but French by way of the country itself, instead of filtered through the lens of a Louisiana recovering from one war, and preparing for another.

The feeling of knowing this man settled over her like plunging into ice. A wicked shiver clattered her teeth.

She put the handkerchief to her throat, spread her fingers to creep around her neck.

The young man put his hands behind his back as he

studied the clothes on display. His jacket spread open to reveal buttons and lace.

He looked up with a smile, and Simone stepped back with a gasp of cold shock.

Confidence John stood before her. Naught but glass between them.

Her fingers squeezed, and she clamped her lips against a fresh breath. After so long. After so many lies told. He was finally back.

The man squinted. Shook his head.

She realized he couldn't see her. Her face was in shadow, making her just an old maid widow shopping on the street.

And the young man wasn't Confidence John. He was the age John had been when last they were together.

She was still without him.

Tears filled her eyes, and the young man swam in her vision. It was like watching a fish dart away under the ripples 'neath the river.

The man tipped his head in salute, then turned away.

Simone squeezed until her forearm ached. The world turned gray.

Behind her, the coach regained motion, finally clear of the fluttering birds and their affected fear. The men had been given the opportunity to act out the farce of protecting the ladies, their honor intact.

Light hit the glass, and the interior of the shop was again replaced with a reflection of the town spreading out toward the sea.

Confidence John stood at her shoulder.

She held her throat tightly enough to trap the scream inside her. Fingers unclenched as she spun and threw her arms wide, and he took her into him.

But this man wasn't Confidence John, either.

Her mind was slowed by the dragging weight of memory, and her fear that without purpose, she would succumb to the past. Old habits.

She was in the arms of her own Jefferson Atwell. For the first time, she understood the depth of her attraction to him. Like the man in the store, Jefferson looked like Confidence John.

He was a good man. He loved her dearly, but like a girl marrying a man just like her father, Simone knew the truth was in Jefferson's face and body. His stance, and the sound of his voice.

She was drawn to him because he reminded her of a man that fed her self-loathing fantasy of redemption.

"My dear, you are a sight. Whatever could have treated you so?"

She pulled away and looked up. Most were too polite to point out their difference in age, but she could see it in the eyes of everyone that eyed them together.

She had done things that could be called noble. Attempts to atone for sins that only she knew about. Jefferson loved her, even knowing the things she allowed herself to admit.

She could still feel her own fingers digging into the skin of her throat. She dabbed her face with the handkerchief. "You deserve better."

His concern became a confused smile. "I have more than I deserve, now. I have not the energy for *better*."

She snorted laughter as she raised the cloth to cover her face. His joke had caught her off guard.

She waved her other hand like shooing a fly away from her hair. He grinned and captured her fingers in a gentle grip, drew her hand to his chest. Then he glanced up the street and ducked his head toward the rough wall of the storefront.

She let him lead her to stand under the store's awning. She wanted to make sure her face wasn't a state, but the thought of looking at her reflection made her queasy. Jefferson would tell her if anything were amiss.

As if seeing into her mind, he dropped down to level their eyes. Patted her lashes with a gentle thumb. Another quick glance to either side, and he pressed her for a kiss.

He often did this. Flaunting convention to assure the world of his love. It pained her that he needed to, but of course he did.

She knew he loved her, and she would receive it if he offered. His kiss, his embrace, and his love.

Selfish old woman.

The kiss became more than was proper in public, and she broke it with a smile. Her palms added soft pressure against his shoulders.

He breathed in through his nose. Slow, like a man taking in an exotic bouquet. "Now, then. What has you in such a state?"

She almost told him then. Of the ghost she had twice seen. Instead, she stepped to the side and turned away to look back at him over her shoulder. The muscles in her neck were tender where she had choked herself. "There was a young man staring at me through the window."

He stiffened and drew back, and the flush of anger that colored his face made her breathless with a fresh wave of laughter.

He took a single stride. Encircled her arm with fingers that tightened like a noose and pulled her around to face him. Pain made her hiss the laughter back through her teeth.

"Show me that man," he snarled.

"Why Jefferson, he's surely gone."

He pulled her close, and she had to push onto her toes.

It felt like he would pull her arm right from her body if she resisted.

"You *show* me."

Lord, the passion in his voice. The pain his hand was causing. She loved it all, but hated herself for needing it. He shook her, and she groaned, closing her eyes and leaning against him. "He couldn't see me against the sun. I was just startled to see him."

She worked her free hand between them to grab his wrist. "Darling, you're hurting me."

He put his mouth against her ear. "Why do this to me? Work me up so?"

His scars were as deep as hers. She knew he wanted to hurt inside. Needed it. Just like her.

He dropped his hand, and she put her face into his chest. Wrapped her arms around his waist. His big hands flattened on her shoulder blades.

She felt his voice vibrate into the bones of her skull. "You know what happens when I do. Ain't never been able to stop. Especially with you. My God, *especially*."

She turned her head away. In the shade of an oak tree stood a nun. Her eyes glinted in the shadows of her habit, like diamonds at the bottom of a dark sack.

Simone tensed, and Jefferson squeezed her in response. "I want to take you right now. Back to when it was just us after the Timbers battle."

The nun stared without blinking. Pale hair curled across her forehead. In the same way that she'd been sure she'd seen Confidence John in the window, Simone was sure she knew this woman.

Jefferson's sigh washed heat across her face. "Take you back and have my fill of you."

She pushed away from him. Flapped her hands for quiet as she sucked her teeth in annoyance.

Jefferson looked down at her in confusion. Followed her gaze and stood straight up at her side.

The nun remained like a dark pillar, and Simone saw the shine of teeth. A grin. One she was sure she had seen many times in the past.

Despite the brim of his hat hanging on his brow, Jefferson shielded his eyes. "Why does she smile so?"

"I don't know," Simone said.

"She seems a piece of memory. Like a taste from years gone."

Simone looked up in shock. How could he see it, too?

The chattering lady birds passed them on the walk as they entered the shop. She cast her disapproving gaze over their self-indulgent horde, jealous. She would never be that young again.

When she and Jefferson turned back to the street, the nun was gone, but Simone still felt the woman's gaze like a point of heat on her back.

Jefferson chuckled. "Emotion ain't never been a thing to *sharpen* the wits."

"Perhaps not."

His arm fell across her shoulder, and she shivered under its weight. He pulled her against him as if shielding her from the cold. "I believe I'll still ask Father Alonso about yonder nun, however. After I send Hatken a-looking."

She nodded against him. "I think that would be best."

"Then we can talk about the man in the window some more."

"Of course."

Two conversations she suddenly wanted nothing to do with.

Chapter Five

EMILY HAD HEARD about a woman in St. Augustine who would take in the socially-displaced. Miss Simone. A local legend with a pet project held together by her widow's dowry.

She could not believe it was her mother. Would not.

But the woman's description was a match to her memory. The town and its people were being fleeced by a confidence artist with a life of practice behind her.

That would make it easy for Emily. If her mother, Miss Simone, was truly working, then they could have a relationship based on a buy-in. Like any good poker game, one just had to figure out the other's price.

Or what they were willing to pay in turn.

But every story illustrated a woman virtuous and true, beloved by many families still holding county property. Emily didn't know this person she heard about. She only knew the woman her mother had been upon leaving home. Bitter and wasted. Mean and lonely. Mourning the loss of a man with a soul as black as her own.

Emily had long since given up crying for the little girl she had been. She could never recover her innocence. Or smile free of pain. Confidence John may have been the cause, but Simone Bisset had been the catalyst. Emily would reconcile what she remembered with what she knew to be true.

These stories were part of a ruse. Miss Simone was a spider and her school was a web, her victims were baited by the fairy tale put forth about a woman who cared about others more than herself.

While in the store, Emily bought a new hat, brown and wide-brimmed, akin to those worn by the drovers and farmers in the plantations — work since pushed away by homes and industry.

She also bought a matching pair of soft leather gloves.

And a new set of suspenders.

She stood in the dark interior with sun glinting through the dust in front of the store windows, waiting for the store's proprietor to fetch her change. The face of the woman she'd come for rested in shadowed contrast to the bright sunlight over her shoulder that sparkled against the stray hairs flying out of her tight bun. Even though she couldn't see her eyes, her sharp cheekbones and wide mouth told the truth. Emily knew.

In spite of the stories, Miss Simone was still just Mama. Not the woman discussed all over the county.

She followed her mother down the silent streets in the early morning, in and out of the light beaming between buildings.

Yet it wasn't doubt that kept her from approaching immediately. It was the nun.

The nun who, all morning, kept appearing in the corner of Emily's eye. Underneath the oak tree. In a dark doorway. Her shadow on the cobbles as she disappeared around a corner.

Who would be following her? Who knew who she was and where she had been going?

It soon became apparent that the nun wasn't following *her*, but her mother.

And the mystery deepened.

Emily's fingers tightened on the gloves until the leather creaked. She looked out the window and smiled, but she wasn't looking at her mother anymore. Her gaze was over Simone's shoulder, into the shaded face of the nun staring back from across the street.

A carriage roared to a halt behind her, blocking Emily's view. A man walked up from the left, concern stark on his face.

Emily accepted her change and asked the shopkeeper to hold her purchases until she returned. She had satisfied herself with watching her mother for the morning. She would follow the nun instead.

He smiled when he took her order into his hands. Made brushing contact with her fingertips.

She grinned at him under the brim of her new hat. It made her jaw ache. Her cheeks threatened to spasm. An innocent gesture, but one she couldn't help but see a sinner's paradise inside.

When she asked for a different exit than the door that opened onto the street, he grinned back and tilted his head toward a short hallway off the rear, containing a bench along one wall with the worn toes of boots peeking out like the wagging tongues of dogs in a row.

Emily saluted him in thanks and left by the back door, emerging into a clay alley covered in a layer of damp straw. She rounded the corner in time to see the nun spin away beneath the rustling leaves of her hiding place. She darted through a gap between the tree and the adobe wall beside it. Headed north.

Emily turned on her heel and walked back toward the back door of *RICARDO'S FASHION CLOTHIER*. Down the alley past several more buildings, where she crossed the street behind a pair of fish carts laden with dripping wares. Along a wall clad in cedar shakes much like those covering her rented bathhouse. When she stepped into the sun at the edge of a goat pen, a twirl of black cloth caught her eye as the nun stooped to pat a lamb's head, pushing its snout through the split rails.

Her habit had fallen, like a hood thrown back after the storm had passed. Emily felt a cold shock so deep, it was as if it arose from her bones.

The nun was the image of memory — an exact reproduction of what her mother had looked like when she was younger. The face she learned to hate as a little girl. Emily was rooted to earth while her mind tried to make sense of this woman.

The nun — that woman that looked like her mother's past twin — stood with a giggle. She waved at the little lamb before bouncing away to mount the wooden stoop of a small house bordering a magnolia garden.

The smell of lemons and salt blew into Emily's face as she stepped back to lean her shoulder against the cedar wall. Hunger gurgled a protest in her belly, but she crossed her arms against it and tipped her head down to watch from under her hat.

She waited for her mother's younger self to come back out.

It wasn't long before a prickle at the back of her neck made here aware that she was being studied from a corner. Was the nun back?

Emily bent to pick a long strand of decorative grass

from a flower box at the foundation of the house next door. And there she saw him, at the edge of her gaze. A man poorly hidden in the arched doorway of a gated courtyard.

Eyes like chiseled coal.

She pinched the grass between her teeth. Looked up at the sky with a grin and pushed off the wall. Shrugged her shoulders and shook her head.

An act of surrender for the watcher in the courtyard.

She saw the eyes draw back into the shadows. As she walked with a casual gait toward the watcher's position, she felt a rising outrage. Whoever he was, he was unconcerned with discovery. Apparently, she was of no concern to this person.

Emily flicked the grass from her teeth. He was was about to be made aware of their mistake.

She swung the iron gate wide and stepped into the courtyard as if she were used to walking this route every day. She passed the watcher, giving him a view of her back and covering her reach into her vest with an adjusting shrug. Snapped her lapels straight with a knife nestled in each palm. Hummed a few notes of "Yankee Doodle."

Intent on acting her part of the confidence game, she remembered the redcoat soldier in New York singing at the top of his cracking voice over a fourth pint of ale.

Her act had done him in. Just as it was about to do for her watcher.

She heard the scrape of a toe behind her: a patch of sand ground under a soft sole. The scents of cedar and safe announced her watcher's approach.

An instinct she had long ago learned to never question made her drop and spin to the left. The devil's hand — most people were unprepared to protect on their non-dominant side.

The tip of her pivoting foot lifted to plant her weight on the heel. Rear leg extended back to plant the toe.

She swung under the watcher's extended hands.

A practiced strike that had ended a hundred conflicts in the past penetrated nothing but a buckskin hem.

The watcher was an Indian. He dodged her strike with a grace that belied the effort, and his breath washed past her face. Whiskey and pepper.

She pulled her slash. Raised her right arm in a guard that put her forearm in front of her face. The rear toe dug into a crack in the cobbles, and her lunge was as perfect as her Louis could ever have wanted.

And still the Indian managed to escape the hit.

He turned into her wrist and chopped down with the heel of his hand.

She dropped the knife in her left hand before he could make contact, near their feet, where she had a chance to recover it instead of seeing it spin into a corner.

She dropped her right elbow. Dipped away from his roll. Changed her hold on the knife in her right hand to an edge-out reverse grip.

The Indian finished his chop, but her soft hand didn't rebound as he expected, and he followed through with an awkward stumble instead of rising up with a hold on her wrist.

The knife she had aimed at his throat carved a shimmering arc of reflected light through the air, but yet again, he avoided a blow that would have easily killed a hundred other men.

His near hand shot up to direct her blow to his outside. The blade split skin on the side of his hand, but the point fell to the side. He had deflected her strike, but he was on one knee. Off balance, with her inside his defenses.

She brought her near foot forward. Without weight

behind it, there would be little force if she connected, but the target itself was important. Aimed at his balls, it had the intended effect. His instincts snapped his legs together, and he threw himself away from her with his arms wide, fingers splayed as if catching sunlight.

His long black hair flowed from his head like glowing oil. A white streak sparkled like a fresh swipe of paint from his forehead. Not just in his hair, but it trailed down his face, and she noticed more splotches as he fell.

On his neck. Down his arms.

He was a handsome man. Perfect in shape and symmetry, but the pale spots added an exotic flair that made him beautiful.

She stared into his face as he fell, and as their gaze met, she hesitated.

Instead of following him down and dropping her weight on his belly — pounding the nail of her blade into his heart — she bounded back into a guard position.

Caught her breath and allowed the Indian to scramble back.

He rolled away to come up on fingers and toes. He spread his stance and stood with his hands held out in front of him.

Instead of reaching for a weapon or preparing a charge, he folded his hands over his heart and bowed his head. "Well met."

Perhaps she had been hasty. She slid her knife into the sheath under her vest, bent to retrieve the fallen blade, and remained at the ready when she stood. Sheathed the second knife with a nod. "Not much of a thank you, but I agree. And well met, sir."

The Indian grinned, his teeth gleaming like treasure. She had to fight to keep hers behind betraying lips.

He dropped one hand, but kept the other over his

heart. "I do not usually provide such things at once." He spoke like an Indian doing a bad impression of a southern gentleman. Like one of those corn-bred politicians always trying to find favor from the British troops still hiding in the weeds, vying for favor from the crown.

His accent was as big a lie as her outfit.

"I'm Hatken," he said.

Despite it being impolite to ask, she couldn't stop her tongue. It was either offend him with the question, or herself with the grin. "And what does that mean?"

He pulled his hand from his heart and stroked the long strand of colorless hair hanging across his forehead as he chuckled. "It means White One."

Emily looked up at the sky. Anything to shove the man's face from her mind. She wanted to know why he smiled. Not the important thing, like why he was watching the nun, but what was creeping behind his mirth.

She looked back at his face. Avoided eye contact. "My name is Emmet Falcone."

Hatken lifted his shoulders in appreciation. "You are the Falcon?"

She was surprised he had heard of her … or *him* … Instead of the usual bravado, Emily shrugged. "I am."

His brows drew together, and he shook his head. "But you are a woman."

She gasped in shock. Her knees felt like she had fallen feet first into a blacksmith's fire. Sweat sprung out on her lip.

Hatken grinned again. "You handled yourself very well."

She caught herself staring. Took a deep breath, but he continued before she could speak. What could she say, anyway?

"I admit, I underestimated you because I didn't think a

woman capable of besting me." He swept his arm up to indicate her costume. "Despite your peacock's feathers."

She heard her own voice ask a hundred different questions. A hundred different denials danced across her mind. But Emily could only whisper. "How did you know?"

"How could I not?"

She spread her arms. "You saw more than this?"

"I saw enough … but now I'm thinking I didn't."

She couldn't stop the smile this time. "Are you asking to see more?"

He dabbed at the blood drying on the side of his hand. Silver buttons glittered beside the rusty smear on his brown vest. "I wouldn't mind."

She buttoned her own vest. "I wouldn't mind showing you."

And if he asked, she would. She'd show him more than he could imagine.

But Hatken shook his head. "I can't. I must ask instead why you are here."

She decided not to lie to this man, even though she'd considered him an enemy only moments ago. No one had ever seen through her disguise before.

She removed her new hat and smoothed the bill in her callused hands. "I'm here to find Simone Bisset."

His expression remained easy, but muscles bunched along his jaw. "And why do you want to do that?"

Emily lost control of her lips, and they split into a grimace. It must look like a leering death mask. "Because she's my mother."

Hatken nodded, surprising her with his lack of shock. His eyes grew thoughtful and distant. "I see it in you. More him than her, but she's there. Miss Simone is the best I've ever known. No wonder you were able to do to me as you did."

The shock was all hers. Hatken extended his hand, and she took it on fingers that felt like melting ice. He pulled her into motion. Led her from the courtyard, and if anybody stared at two men — a white man and a scarred Indian — holding hands in the street, Emily never noticed.

Chapter Six

SIMONE BRUSHED chalk from her apron, only to leave bright streaks behind. She held her hands out and turned from the blackboard, where she had written:

As the twig is bent, so is the tree inclined.

Buford sat in his customary seat in the corner, a creaky chair that gave him a view of every entrance into the front room of her school. Having him keep watch was the only way she felt comfortable turning her back on the windows.

He was such a quiet man, and she had long since convinced herself to be satisfied with the little history he had trusted her with. He had converted to Catholicism to earn his freedom from Spain, and even though she had heard him quote the scripture in English *and* Latin, she had never seen him attend service.

Father Alonso had long since stopped asking about his absence on Sundays.

Buford dressed like an accountant loosening the restrictions of the collar for a casual dinner at home. She suspected he had affected the dress from his former owner.

She had once edged around asking outright, but he had only shaken his large head.

"They are gone." His soft voice had trembled with emotion. Mourning or regret, she couldn't tell.

She had placed her hand over his heart, a touch that surprised them both. She asked if he ever feared being followed, and again he shook his head.

"There are no more."

He had taken her hand from his chest and held it like it was made of rice paperas his fierce gaze filled with tears. "I killed them *all*."

Then he fled from the room with hurried stomps, and she'd never asked again. Sometimes a secret hurt more to keep than to tell.

As they should.

She showed him her dusty palms and shrugged with a chuckle, but his face stopped her short. Narrowed eyes and tense jaw as his gaze flicked to the front window. A shadow darkened the glass.

He leaned forward to plant his feet on the floor, and his right hand slipped to the gap between the buttons on his burgundy vest.

Simone leaned back as if she had forgotten something, positioning herself behind the small lectern and laying her hands flat on the handle of that Spanish dagger living the top shelf. Father Alonso had assured her it was genuine *Albacete* steel from *Castilla la Mancha*. But she cared not for its history.

Only for the feel of it in her hand.

Hatken emerged in the aura of sunlight, hand extended to the front door handle, bell jingling as he stepped through.

She lifted her hands from the shelf, and just barely stopped herself from rubbing her palms across her apron again. A *tsk* of frustration as she stepped to the side, welcoming the man back, only to freeze once again.

A face she recognized from ancient memory, confused with a recent sighting. The young man from the window followed the Indian inside.

And Simone was a young woman again. Dancing on the back of a wagon as John sauntered around the fire to look up at her from the small crowd.

She fluttered her eyelids. Pulled her attention away from memory to look at Buford. He stood to intercept Hatken as the young Indian crossed to sit in a chair along the front of the side wall.

Hatken flapped his hands in a gesture meant to slow an animal, calm and sure. He dropped to his seat, and Buford eyed the stranger before lowering himself back to his chair.

The stranger with the familiar face stopped at the last row of backless chairs. The silence of the his arrival yawned, and she was unwilling to break it. Dread filled her breast. She felt as if she had lost her balance mid-stride.

Jefferson entered the tableau, holding his hat in front of his chest.

"What do y'all say?" he asked, and his voice was a tensioned spring.

Simone snuck her gaze up to glance at the stranger, and her eyes widened in shock to find him staring right at her. She caught her breath and looked at Jefferson, unable to muster the words to start.

Hatken leaned back and crossed his arms. He shrugged and pulled one hand free to point at the stranger. "I went out to follow the nun."

"I was gonna ask you to do that," Jefferson said. "I thank you."

Simone heard his words soften and broaden, a thickening of his accent. He was concentrating on his temper instead of his diction.

"I tell you, she's no nun. She wants to be seen too much. Nuns always hide." He looked up and gestured at the ceiling. "Like God is constantly watching."

"I'm wondering less about the nun and more about the fella standing in my house," Jefferson replied.

The stranger looked at the ceiling. At the corners, tracking them to the floor. Finally, he looked at Jefferson. "*Your* house, is it?"

His voice sent a tingle down her spine. Not *exactly* like John's. Too high. Less gravel. But just as assured., with a playfulness that hinted at secrets. Was he a son? Confidence John was widely known.

Simone took a tiny step and her heel hit the wood planks like a driven nail. "No, it belongs to me."

Jefferson's jaw bulged, but he made no move to correct her or defend himself.

The stranger turned back like he had to push his gaze through air that resisted. Like it was an effort to look at her. "He did seem a little young."

Jefferson leaned forward. "Now you wait right there."

Hatken raised both hands in a chopping motion. Simone saw a line of drying blood smeared along the outside of his left palm. "You cannot win against *this* one, Mr. Jefferson. I have the shame of it."

"Who *are* you?" Jefferson asked.

Hatken answered for the stranger. "She is the Falcon."

Confused silence settled over the parlor, and Simone looked from face to face. There was obvious knowledge in the name, but she didn't share it. "*Who* is the Falcon?"

Jefferson shook his head as if coming awake. "A killer."

She had known many killers over the years.

Buford sat up straight and buttoned his vest. "A butcher."

That was a little worse.

Hatken tipped his head toward the stranger, like he was appreciating a fine jewel. "An artist."

The stranger's face flushed with embarrassment. It looked like an act. He ducked his head exactly as she expected, and spread his hands. "Let me tell you who I am."

He bent to drop his hat on the nearest seat. As he stood, knife in his hand, appearing as if by magic.

Hatken looked on with an odd expression of pride. "You see?"

The stranger's mouth twitched in a suppressed smile, and before Simone could ask another questions, the stranger began his tale.

"I have learned what I have learned so I can kill a man." His accent was alluring. Not quite anything, but with a romantic cadence. Intimate. His teeth pressed together in a bitter grin. "And that man is my father. My entire youth … *Si jeunesse savait, si viellesse pouvat*, yes? Almost my entire life until now, and I think I am ready."

Simone dared not ask for a translation. She was transfixed, as were the rest of them, and her dread grew.

The stranger lifted his arms, and revealed a knife in his other hand. She resisted the urge to clap.

He tapped the blades together, and they chimed like distant bells. "A hellish childhood put me on this path. Watching my mother abused by men who would use her for a purpose a young mind could not understand, until it started happening to me, too. And she never prepared me … or protected me."

Simone hated that mother immediately. Thought of her own lost daughters, who she'd failed in much the same way. It was a familiar hate, because she'd long felt it for herself. But her sympathy drowned her shame, and she forced her hands from her own throat, lacing them over the stain of chalk on her apron.

The stranger twirled the knives between his fingers, and they rang with music.

"It is desperate, the pain of a child. There is no way to measure its depth until much later, and by then, any damage done is covered by years of living. Layer after layer of varnish until the truth only shows through the cracks. Like the scorpion that scurries from the parched earth to feel the sun."

Buford's chair creaked as he leaned forward. He held a thick finger up, and it trembled as he pointed at Hatken. "He said *she* was the Falcon."

The stranger nodded with another terrible grin. "That's right."

The blades rang together, and Simone stepped back on shaking legs.

The stranger extended his arms while rotating the blades until they pointed back at his chest. Like he was offering her the weapons to use against him. "It is not always the sins of the father that are visited upon the son."

And Simone knew.

The stranger ... her daughter ... pulled the knives in until the tips were pressed into the fabric of her vest. As if she would stab herself at Simone's command. "No. Sometimes, it's the sins of the *mother*."

Simone's vision dimmed to a dull gray; her ears roared with the sound of her own heart. Even as a small girl, Emily had looked just like her father. To see her grown into a copy of him made Simone's guts twist as if poisoned.

She took an unsteady step back. Her other foot

followed, and her shoulder erased the words from the blackboard as she leaned against it for support.

Emily shrugged. She seemed saddened that Simone hadn't taken the knives from her. Plunged them into her own heart, or maybe into her daughter's. She slid the blades away, and Simone didn't see where they had gone. Their glimmer disappeared as if they had never existed.

In place of the knives was a small book, stained and battered. Simone knew at once what it was.

Confidence John's journal. The story of his obsession with her. With cards. With killing.

Another step took her into the doorway of the kitchen, and when the jamb blocked her view of the book held out in her daughter's hand, Simone found the strength to run.

Chapter Seven

HER MOTHER HAD REFUSED the knives. The book. Even her own daughter.

She watched Simone spin away in a whirl of petticoats and chalk dust, and the weight of the book became too much. It dragged her arm back down. Slipped from her fingers to hit the floor with a flat clap like a gunshot.

The big man — he looked like a military man trying to settle into life after war — jumped into motion, taking a halting step toward Simone's departure, then stopped and turned to Emily. He wanted answers to questions he didn't know how to ask.

She felt the same way. She wanted to follow Simone and demand … something.

Emily would have laughed if not for her own pounding heart. Her identity first discovered, and then *revealed*. She could never hide in front of these people. Not now that they knew what she really was.

But then again, *she* didn't even know what she was anymore.

Maybe Hatken was the problem. It was a near-constant

struggle to keep her gaze away from where he sat. She couldn't help but be aware of his attention on her, aware of his quiet admiration. He was in her *senses*.

She met his eyes, and he blinked away his confusion, but when he opened his mouth to speak, nothing came out. He looked like a fish struggling without water to breathe, and she barely stifled her laughter.

Or her tears. Sometimes, they felt the same.

She straightened her cuffs. Smoothed her vest and coat. Felt the reassuring weight of all the steel hidden on her body.

She wasn't sure what he was waiting for, but he seemed to believe she could take care of herself, so she relaxed and met his accusing gaze.

"Who the hell are you?"

"My name is Emmett Fal — *Emily* Falcone. A long time ago, I was Emily Bisset."

The black man edged around the ex-soldier to extend a respectful hand. "My name is Buford, and I see the resemblance."

Emily took his hand in a firm grip, and though her fingers had been trained for years to hold the saber, his felt like they could crush rock. She nodded with a small dip of her head. "Should I assume you mean no offense by that?"

Instead of answering, Buford released her hand and stepped back. He swept his arms to the side to indicate the ex-soldier. "And this is Jefferson Atwell."

Jefferson didn't offer his hand. He brushed his fingers against his hat brim in salute. "I help run the place."

Emily shrugged. "After you inherit her property, will you no longer *help*?"

His face flushed with blood. Ruddy color bloomed along his jawline. "What's that supposed to mean?"

Buford gestured toward Hatken. "And it seems you two have already met."

Jefferson pressed forward. "I asked you a question."

"I am telling you, Mister Jefferson. She is the finest I saw."

Emily wasn't sure if she had only imagined there had been a stress added to the word *finest*, but maybe ... She cursed herself for distraction. Focused on the heaving bull in front of her. "I heard your question, sir. But your anger shows me that I have no need to answer it."

Jefferson took a measured breath through his nose. "You think I'm only with her for what? Status and money? Like them war boys who come home to nothing but a bunch o' widows in need of a man? Is that what you think?"

Emily buttoned the bottom of her coat. Made a show of primping the pleats and folds of her outfit. "*Is it?*"

Jefferson glanced to the side for support from his friends, but Buford was looking at her boots. No ... he was looking at the fallen journal.

"Them spinsters line up on the docks," Jefferson continued, "and they wait for a young man to come home. One that's seen a little that brung him up from the boy he left as. Kids and all, they wait. And them ol' boys fall right into line to marry. A ready-made family with an inheritance built right in, but let me tell you something. I fought *hard* to court that woman, cuz she was suspicious of any advances made by me or any other man seeking her bed."

Emily nearly choked. If this man only knew the number of men that had shared her bed.

"And don't think for a single minute that I don't know what she done, cuz unlike you, I know what she done *after* all that, and she's one of the best I've ever known."

Emily had been gone for so long — could a person

really change? Or could a person really act as if she had changed?

"Do you love my mother?"

Jefferson nodded, and his shoulders sagged. "Yes sir, I do. More than she'll let me, and it breaks my heart."

Emily could only breathe in small gasps. Like a child trying not to cry.

She had fostered a hate in her heart. For her mother first. For her father to fill whatever was left over. And she'd honed that hate with memories of pain and humiliation suffered. Of Simone's unwillingness to protect that which should have been most precious — the innocence of a young life.

Emily looked up at the ceiling. Cracked plaster graying with age. Such a heavy thing to hang over so much fragility.

Fear had been the only thing to keep her moving forward. The fear that she would never find her mother, to tell her how she was going to suffer for what she had done. The fear that she would never find her father, to kill him for setting the path of her future into motion.

The fear of finding love. Of losing it.

The fear of not being worthy of another's love.

And still she had tried to love. First, Louis Cheval, and now, past countless others, she felt the stirring for Hatken.

If only she could stand outside of herself and take her own shoulders, shake herself while screaming into her face to just stop.

She had loved her father, and he had left her scarred. Her love for Louis had left her empty. All the others had just been an attempt to feel real. To exercise a hope more addictive than drink.

And yet, the mother whose abuse had turned her into this was loved?

She glared at Jefferson. "Then why are you wasting your time with me?"

He wilted like a cat in a bath. "What?"

"If you love her, go to her and tell her so. I can attest that there is not a single woman who tires from hearing it."

Emily stepped back, put her hand over her heart and made a half bow over her front foot. "You have my word, sir, as a man of the saber, I will do no harm in your absence."

Jefferson shrugged the coat onto his shoulders. Closed the top with a brass button while he looked at her with narrowed eyes. Calculating but unsure.

Finally, he nodded. "Alright *mister*. I'll see where she's gone, but upon our return, we'll have satisfaction."

Before leaving, he became the country gentleman again. An affectation not as convincing as her own Emmet, but Jefferson seemed to have less discipline for the art. Or maybe less practice.

Hatken stared at her in amused admiration.

Buford kept both hands behind his back. Polite waiting. She mirrored his stance. "And you?"

His grin was a rush of emotion, like he had been waiting his turn in hours of silence. "My only question … Miss Emily?"

She felt the weight of the rice sack between her legs and had to stop herself from rolling her eyes. She nodded instead.

He spoke like a man carefully weighing every syllable. She wondered if his first language was English. I am less interested in your parentage, which sits plainly on your face, and more interested in the book. May I?"

"Be my guest."

Buford picked the book up from the floor and lifted it to his nose as if he were sampling its aroma. He cracked the journal open, and after a moment's study, grinned then handed the book back with an air of excitement. It made the big man seem like a child, and she couldn't help but smile.

"I will return directly."

He left on feet made lighter by discovery, and his bouncing gait only enforced the illusion that he was an overlarge child.

She glanced at Hatken.

His grin was open and beautiful, and she returned it on instinct. Neither of them spoke.

Buford returned with an ornate silver disc the size of both his open hands held against his chest. It wasn't until he pointed the object toward her that she realized he was protecting the glass of a mirror.

She offered the journal without comment. He opened the book near the center and held it up so that the page was reflected in the mirror.

"Come see." He included Hatken. "Come."

Emily felt an irrational fear, for some reason hesitant look. Did she want to know

She and Hatken crowded against his left shoulder, and in the mirror were words. Legible English. She looked up into Buford's wide eyes with a growing excitement. But the satisfaction of learning her father's trick cooled as she looked back down to read.

I gave her the other half of my soul and told her to keep it safe.

She cried then, tears blurring the page so she wouldn't have to read any more. She stepped away and wondered how she could ever go on if she couldn't control the emotions that lurked beneath the self she'd painstakingly built over the years.

Then her grief became a freezing balm.

She swiped the tears away with her jacket sleeve. Squinted as she looked through the window.

The nun stood under the shade of the palm tree next to the mission across the street.

As their eyes met, the nun whirled around and disappeared into the shadows.

Emily cleared her throat. "Hatken, would you mind following me, please?"

Chapter Eight

Simone dropped to her bed. Claudia had made the blankets tight at the corners. It was like dropping onto a hard mound of hay, until the down wheezed out air and her body settled into softness.

She buried her face in the comforter, makeup be damned and reached above her until her fingers found the ruffled edges of the pillowcase. She brought the pillow down over the back of her head before she let out a silent scream. Then pushed her face deeper and stared at the bursts of light that bloomed behind her eyelids.

Her lungs burned. Hitched against her ribs. Her shoulders ached with the effort to hold the position of suffocation. Then the panic gave way to comfort. Warm release as she settled into darkness.

She came to in a fuzz of sensation. In the safe blackness under the pillow where nobody could see her. Her fingers tingled as if ants marched along the creases in her skin.

Her old skin.

Still, she hadn't yet outlived her past.

Simone sighed into the mattress where, most nights, she and Jefferson reveled in the warmth of each other, pressed tight like a second skin. She would run her fingers along all his scars to occupy herself in the dark. To keep from seeing all the damage she'd done to herself.

And that was the worst of it. Not what others had done to her, but what she had done to her own mind and body.

Or so she'd thought, until today.

Her greatest pain had just walked through the door, and she hadn't been prepared. So many years convincing herself that Emily was truly gone and punishing herself for driving her away. But somehow her return — dressed like a man, with both her father's countenance and his manners — was even worse.

She thought of her other daughter, given over to a church in a swampy territory too young yet to be a state. Seeing what Emily had become, could she continue to convince herself that the other was so much better off?

Cool air fluttered up the backs of her legs, letting her know that Somebody had entered the room. When the weight pressed into the mattress, and the frame creaked as it settled, she knew it was Jefferson.

Who else would want to be with her right now?

Not her Emily. And after today, perhaps never anyone again.

His hand rested on her back. Just above her bottom rib. A tickle spot.

He would use it if she didn't relent, so she removed the pillowrolled out from under his touch. Sat with her head bowed. "I must be a fright."

"Beautiful as ever."

She glanced at him from the corner of her eyes, through a falling curtain of frizzing hair. His face was so earnest, she still had to fight to ask him to say it again.

Even when she got what she needed, she wanted more.

She didn't care if she *was* wearing shoes, she worked her feet under her and walked on her knees through the treachery of the soft mattress and the useless blankets.

His arms opened to catch her before she fell, and she pressed her face into his chest as she had the bed. His embrace was fierce. Crushing but comforting, though it made her spine creak. All her breath left her, and she clung to him in case he let go.

She could do it. She could accept his love. Punishing him was punishing herself, and perhaps it was time to stop. He didn't deserve to be punished anymore.

Besides, if he said he loved her, and she believed it, only to learn of his lie, how delicious would that pain be?

His voice vibrated through her bones. "Come on, Mone. This may not be the way of it in your dreams, but she's back."

She wasn't quite ready, so she shook her head against him. He grabbed her upper arms and pushed her away. She resisted to the point of pain, but he was too strong.

"You can, you must, and you *will*. I am confounded, I admit, but I said I'd stand by you and I will. You've made me a better man. Lord, you made me a *good* man."

Soft stubble dragged across her palms as she took his face between her hands. A warning in the back of her mind went unheeded when she opened her mouth. "I love you, Jefferson Atwell."

His embrace was gentle this time, and she relaxed into him. Content to feel nothing more than the heat of his breath wash down her neck.

The moment was ruined by raised voices from below. Not in alarm, but more … indignant.

She drew herself out of Jefferson's lap, and they looked at each other with sheepish guilt. This moment should have happened years ago, if not for her selfish … no. She would not do this. Jefferson Atwell was more than the shadow of Confidence John. He deserved her love, for whatever it was worth. Now that she had given it, she realized it had cost her nothing.

She turned to her dressing table and used the milky reflection from the old mirror to pat her hair down, wipe under eyes, pinch her cheeks for color.

She turned away to find Jefferson ducking back in from the hallway. "It sounds like the priest and them are having it out."

"Having it out about what?"

"Sounds like it's about the nun."

She held her hand out, and he took it. Their usual dance felt different now. His grip was accompanied by weight. Surety. The knowledge that she was truly in his hand, and his alone.

She knew it was just her fantasy, a feeling she couldn't define as anything more than dreaming, but knowing that didn't make it any less real.

She sent reassurance into her return squeeze. He led her to the top of the stairs, then held her back before she could place her first foot and put his mouth was next to her ear. "Now you will surely marry me?"

The question shouldn't have surprised her. She leaned back to look up into his eyes. "Of course I will, but not in this dreadful place. Let us move beyond this first."

She hurried downstairs, with Jefferson at her heels. Voices swelled as they passed through the kitchen and into the parlor.

It was indeed Father Alonso. Buford's deep bass, and Emily's male affectation that was so easy to see through, now that she knew.

As she entered the parlor, Hatken and Emily held the

nun between them. All three faced the priest, with Buford at Father Alonso's shoulder. Hatken lifted a finger to point at the ceiling. "You say your god made the sky as well?"

Father Alonso looked from Emily to Hatken, and his forehead creased in frustration. "My son, all of everything is His creation."

Hatken shook his head. "But the sky already *is*."

Buford dropped a big hand on the priest's shoulder, and Father Alonso looked up in alarm. "Father," Buford said. "If you please. My apologies for our savage friend here, his is not a religion as we would know it."

Father Alonso spread his hands. "But what is life without the Word of God?"

Hatken shrugged. "Peaceful? Without blame or shame or the need to get up so early on Sundays?"

Emily hid her chuckle behind her hand, but sobered as Simone and Jefferson came near. Alonso followed her attention, and his face brightened.

"Ah, Miss Simone. Could you please have them unhand this young nun, please? I have not yet called the constable, out of respect for our friendship."

She suddenly hated the man. Despised all her dealings with him, and the leverage he believed he held over her. He barely remembered the names of the people in this building. She knew with a certainty that he didn't know this woman.

Simone released Jefferson's hand with a regret that surprised her. Her hand already missed his touch. "Father Alonso, I ask only this. What is the young nun's name?"

The priest drew back with a smile. Spread his hands. "Why, her name is ... Sister ..." His eyes darted to the nun, but her gaze was on the floor. One corner of her lip twitched in a suppressed smile.

"I must confess, I do not know her, but as she wears the habit, it is my duty to protect those—"

Hatken laughed. "Did you hear that? He *confesses*."

Emily nodded. "I *did* hear that."

They spoke like old friends, comfortable as if they had known one another for years. A peculiarity Simone didn't have time to ponder.

The nun sighed. "I *paid* him."

Father Alonso's brow furrowed in affronted anger. "How dare you—"

"Father Alonso, *please,*" Simone snapped. "Even now, as Spain leaves for your native shore, as you stand before a woman who has long since negotiated for her place inside your scheming house, do you still pretend to play the innocent?"

The priest's stance and demeanor transformed with breathtaking speed, and the priest stood with a haughty disappointment that made Simone feel like a peasant.

"Yes, perhaps it *is* time. Very well, señora. This girl asked for a place in town where she could stay unmolested, and for a small fee, I vouched for her. The habit and her run of the church was a separate transaction."

His lids dropped to hood his eyes, and his tongue darted from his mouth to moisten his lips, completing the illusion that he was somehow a snake.

His smile stretched wider, and he looked at the nun. "Shall I tell them the rest?"

The young woman shrugged and looked out the front window.

Of course this was happening — Simone's sins coming home to roost, just in time to watch her world unravel. The urge to run away fell over Simone again, but she forced herself to stay and face the punishment she so deserved.

She allowed Father Alonso complete his performance,

pulling the habit away from her hair, then dropped it to the floor as if it burned. The fake nun's hair flowed out like sparkling gold. Unlined forehead above blue eyes so pale, they looked silver. Just like hers.

Father Alonso stepped back as if he had just performed a magic trick. "She is—"

"My daughter, of course." Simone gave him a scathing look, full of contempt. Then she turned to Emily's younger sister. "You should have just come to me, Rita."

Her daughters looked at her with identical expressions of satisfaction. As if they could feel her pain. As if they enjoyed it. Like the last time she had seen *his* face.

How Simone wished that she and Confidence John had never met.

Chapter Nine

Emily had released her hold on the little nun's arm without realizing it. Her hands had betrayed her, but Rita — her sister — stood still.

The line of her body under the dark cloth. The color of her hair and eyes. Skin like cream. It was clear that half of her blood belonged to Simone.

Emily felt like a crumpled napkin.

She hadn't seen herself as a woman in so many years. Couldn't remember herself as anything other than a pretty-faced man, honed like any duelist, with muscles like iron beneath skin marred by hard-edged steel.

Still, even with her sister's beauty, their mother had abandoned Rita too. There was enough comfort in the thought for Emily to bite back the jealousy that was suddenly like a hand at her throat.

Father Alonso folded his arms over the protrusion of his belly and looked at Emily with a raised eyebrow. Lips parted in a slight circle.

Emily glanced over at Hatken, but he stood easy with his hand on Rita's arm and his gaze on the priest. Emily looked back to Father Alonso. She crossed her arms in imitation of his own stance. "So, who pays you now?"

The priest flapped his hand in dismissal. "It is not the money that concerns me, young man. It is your face, or rather the face it resembles."

"Careful there, Father."

"No, no, my son. It is a face of renown and infamy. You look like a man I have known, and I could make sense of your presence if I could confirm it."

Rita turned and peered up at Emily's face with narrowed eyes. Hatken let go with a shrug and turned to examine with her.

Emily ignored them both. "I will confirm what I wish, Father."

The priest sucked his teeth. Drew out the suspense with a gap-toothed grin. "You are the image of Confidence John."

"You are actually the first person to pick up on that in all my living years, Father." Let him wonder if she meant it in all sincerity, or in all sarcasm.

"He has been a benefactor of mine and Miss Simone's for many years now. I am very familiar with his ways."

Her mother's benefactor? That seemed a purposefully casual slip of information. Emily stilled her face even as her heart raced. Was she as close as that, then? Did she but have to find her mother? She'd assumed that her father had abandoned them all, but perhaps it was only his daughters he wished to avoid.

"Come now, young man," Father Alonso prodded. "Are you his son?"

"Confidence John Bisset *is* my father."

"Damn," Rita muttered.

"Why damn?" Emily asked. "Were you going to try to have your way with me?"

The priest flapped his sleeves in disapproval. "Such language."

Rita pursed her lips and arched an eyebrow. Emily could see a host of men dropping to their knees to do whatever it took to get that look directed at them.

"Well … *Brother* … I am ashamed to admit that I was."

Emily hated that Simone had damaged Rita so. Simone and the many men that she'd undoubtedly given Rita to as a plaything, after Emily had left.

"Don't fret so, Brother. I'm sure there's someone out there for you. A handsome and strong man like yourself."

"I am not your brother."

Rita thrust her hip out and leaned back. "Come now. We are family."

Emily ignored her sister in favor of the priest. "Yes, I have admitted that Confidence John is my father, but I am not his son."

"My son, I do not understand."

Emily smiled. "That is because I am not your son, either. I am Confidence John's daughter."

The priest drew back as if he had caught a whiff of rotten meat. "What?"

Rita straightened. "The hell you say."

Emily shrugged. "Believe whatever you wish, *Sister*."

When Rita's gaze dropped to her crotch, Emily shook her head. "Naught there but warm rice."

Rita's face twisted with disgust. "I wouldn't have fucked you, anyway."

Father Alonso squealed in distress. Hatken threw his head back and cackled laughter.

And Simone — she looked sad.

Emily saw the fragile beauty flee Rita's face. Chased away by bitter hatred. Her newfound sister planted her fists on her hips and glared up at Hatken. "What are you laughing at, crow? I wouldn't fuck *you* for heaven."

Father Alonso's face glowed like a red shuttered lamp, and he lifted his hands, beseeching his congregation of three. "My children, please!"

Hatken wiped his eyes and looked down at Rita with sympathy. "Oh, little rabbit. You cannot make me angry, for I am satisfied with my soul, and you are not the woman for this one."

Rita snarled, "What would you know? You're just an ignorant savage."

Hatken shrugged. "So I am to hear."

Rita smoothed her robes, and even through the thick black fabric, the body that seemed to have served her well in the past was quite evident. The priest stared open, his offense at their language forgotten.

Rita's snarl became a sweet smile. "What woman would have you, anyway?"

Hatken turned away, and Emily caught her breath when his gaze met hers. He lifted a shoulder in an embarrassed shrug. "I hope *she* will."

Rita's cruel laugh would have cut if Emily wasn't captured by Hatken's stare. His dark eyes seemed like water pails, and the memory of a dead man's eyes looking up from the bottom of a well flashed through her mind.

A man for a man. One taken before she could save him, and one to take her before she could save herself.

Her own need for love cut deeper than any word from her sister, no matter how much suffering had tempered the blade of her tongue.

"Oh, Lord," Rita said. "She's good at being a man, I'll give her that, but she's her father's daughter. My dear sister will make a poor woman."

Hatken smiled. "I am satisfied with *her* soul as well."

Emily refused to look away. "Hatken, you don't know me."

"I know your mother."

Emily wanted to understand. He loved her mother, but the woman she remembered was so different from the one this man knew. "I'm not certain of that."

Could there be even more siblings struggling through a past of similar misfortune, sired on Simone, or other women just like her? Who else sought Confidence John?

And what if someone else found him first?

Rita sidled up to Father Alonso with her hands clasped before her.

A pretty little thing ready to break a man's heart.

She put her little hand on the priest's shoulder. "I must tend to myself."

Father Alonso's face twitched in annoyance. He seemed to have been caught up in private reverie, and it looked like he didn't appreciate the interruption. Emily forestalled him with a firm shake of her head. "I'll take her."

"Absolutely not. I want to be escorted by a man. And not by some scarred runaway outcast." She glared at Hatken, turned to the priest. "Am I a prisoner?"

He shook his head as if the very thought were offensive. "Of course not, my child."

Emily spread her coat to expose her vest. "Maybe not, but it would be a fine thing to have you in sight."

"You don't trust a man of the cloth?"

Emily snorted laughter at Rita's sneering insinuation. "Not a one."

Father Alonso stepped between the sisters. "I beg your pardon, young man."

"She has told you," Hatken interjected. "She is not a man."

The priest stomped his foot. "That will be quite

enough. It would not do to have a man escort a young woman — a young woman in the garb of a nun — to the … *bathroom.*"

"We're family, as she has already said."

"Recently discovered family, young man." As the priest handed Rita the rest of her disguise, Emily took a measured breath.

Rita seemed to feel safe with the priest, so she gave in. "Take her, Father. But I want your word she will return. We have business to discuss."

The glint of greed flickered through the priest's eyes. "And what do you think my word is worth?"

Emily looked at Rita. "A man of the cloth, huh?"

Rita shrugged and slid the habit over her head. Tucked the stray hairs behind the opening her face was too small for.

Emily stepped back and scrubbed her hands together. "I care now less than I did, which makes your word worth less than it was."

Father Alonso held his arm out, and Rita ducked underneath to press herself into the priest's side. "And such is the way of it. *Chau, Señor* Bisset."

With Rita matching him step for step, he led her under the jingling bell of the front door.

She felt Hatken's gaze on her as she watched them disappeared into the dark through the mission's side door.

But only after Simone excused herself to the kitchen, to give instructions for breakfast, and Jefferson followed, did Emily turned to face him.

She looked at his feet. "You must understand, it has been a long time since I knew my mother, and there is a deep hatred for the person she was. The people we *both* were. My father and …"

Acting was so easy. This was terrible, for she'd never had any talent for the truth.

"I don't know the woman you do," she confessed. "I don't even know the woman I am."

Hatken stepped forward and took her hand, as freely as he had before, when he'd brought her here. She had never met *anyone* like him. She pulled him closer, and he didn't resist. Anyone who happened to pass by would see two young men in close conversation. But she feared for what might happen if they were spied doing aught else.

She saw herself, small and distorted, in the reflection of his dark eyes. "I would like to learn about both of those women."

He bowed his head. "I would like to teach you."

Chapter Ten

SIMONE SWATTED Jefferson's hands away. His need to comfort had gone from charming protection to obsessive smothering. She couldn't think with his presence pushing into her. She wanted to hide. To treat her wounds in private. Or perhaps to escape while no one watched.

"Mone, please." His pet name sounded like a command, and she turned her back on him. Clutched the journal and closed her eyes.

She took a deep breath that smelled like him. "Jefferson, darling. May I be alone?"

She worried for his ego. Feared to anger him. She dropped the journal on the rumpled bed. Spun out from under his hands and pressed against him. A damsel in distress, closing her eyes against her lie.

She just wanted him gone. He was too much. Like trying to take in the whole horizon at once.

He wrapped her in an embrace far more gentle than she deserved. Lowered his mouth to her ear. "Tell me. What can I do?"

She fought the urge to scream in frustration, and

her fingers curled into fists full of the rough fabric of his coat. "You can do nothing. I just … I need a *moment*. Darling …" She pushed herself away to look up into his worried eyes. She couldn't say what she knew he wanted to hear, but she came close. "My love."

He smiled and stood up straight. "I will do *anything* for you. Always would have."

He was a child in a killer's body, as fragile as she herself. That was why they fit together so well.

Like the teeth of an opposing comb settling into the gaps of the other.

She took his hands in hers and brought them to her lips. "We are to be married, sir. A few minutes is nothing to wait for with forever on the other side."

He nodded. Reluctant to agree. "Yes, ma'am."

"Then go. I'll be there directly." And regardless of how much she wanted to run away, she told him the truth. "I'll never leave you."

She worried that he would take more convincing, but he pulled his hands away and turned to leave. The door latched with a soft click behind him.

And she was alone.

Despite how much she may have wanted it a moment ago, the empty room suddenly felt too big. She took a step to the door, but she stopped before she could touch the doorknob or call Jefferson back.

She would no longer chase the thing she wanted. Not before finding the thing she needed.

She turned around to look at the book. The journal of a man who had changed and ruined and … even bettered so many lives.

Her letters to him had all been stories of success. Improvement and victory. It was all he wanted to hear while he holed up on his island, the guns of the Spanish Navy keeping him safe.

Rich as a desert prince.

She spent years spending his money on an existence desperate for significance., terrified to seek out the daughters they had both destroyed. Drowning her guilt in salvation, but never her own.

It was dangerous for him to leave *El Halconito*. Too many men wanted him dead. Too many women wanted the same. Including, apparently, one of his own daughters.

John praised Simone for her efforts helping those less fortunate, and she always felt like it was a pat on her head. Dismissive.

She'd been one of his favorites, and now he placated her with gold to fund her pet project, like a rich wife with nothing to do but decorate a large house. Staying out of the important man's way.

She picked up the journal and opened it.

She remembered watching him, bent over the light of a candle reflecting in the mirror he used when shaving. His squinted eyes peered into the other book while he wrote.

So many secrets.

But his letters had been written plain for anyone to see. Love letters from a twisted man who still thrilled at the idea of evil fantasy. He'd detailed every abuse he still dreamed of inflicting on her, and she read every word out of what she believed to be duty.

It was really because his words, no matter how cruel, made her feel … real. The only thing that proved she existed was the pain he was freely willing to cause.

Then she had met Jefferson, damaged in a northern battle against an enemy he would never tell her about — she only saw what they had done to him.

He was so powerful. Body and mind of iron, but in her

arms, he was small and weak. An emotional fragility she recognized.

And she saw the way out through him.

As her relationship with Jefferson intensified, the letters grew more infrequent. Almost as if he was watching.

His final letter had been curt. No details, only polite phrases with a tacit finality that brought tears to her eyes. Like he was stepping down to get out of the other man's way.

But the money never stopped. And that was what convinced her that Confidence John still loved her. The reason she had been so unwilling to accept Jefferson's adoration.

She flipped the curling pages to the last entry and carried the journal to the mirror over her wash basin. It took several moments to get the angle right, but with the whole page in view, she could read every word.

The Third Of October — I am finally done with it. Done with her. I must leave this life behind. This errant journey that does nothing but distract from my main focus.

I will retire to El Halconito. Count Raphael has assured me of a future I could only dream about in youth.

Yet, I am torn. Between this life of inevitable conclusion, and the one I have pursued with dogged passion. My secret desire. A woman of an appetite to match my own. Not a woman purchased. Bribery and reward. But a woman who wants me because she wants what I am.

I can no longer fool myself as Simone had fooled me these many years. I cannot abide by her addiction or her lies. There are some things a man must never bear.

The greater lie that she is beyond the poppy is the falsehood of another daughter. This one left at a mission near the border of Georgia.

I have found her, in spite of Simone's pale attempts to keep her a secret, and I must say, she is an image of her mother. Perhaps as a family united, there could be a chance of happiness.

Compliant daughters and mother under my roof. But alas, that bliss is not to be known.

A perverse desire to keep us together still grips me, and I will stoke those coals with money. And I will send the same as a dowry for my daughters that will never know me, for one had fled my hand, and the other knows it not.

Father Carlos will hold this personal treasure for any of these little women that deign to follow my clues, but Father Mateo in Santa Lucia will hold my daughters' treasure. Buried under the church foundation.

Or perhaps that money will be lost to time. It is no matter to me, for the only woman I have ever loved can never be mine.

I will be a man of many pleasures, but always alone. And not without dreams.

The words blurred as she pulled the journal away from the glass.

This?

Simone lowered the book and looked into the reflection of her own eyes. This was the mystery?

Absence from the man had changed her perception of him. Her memory of him was not quite as … trite as the man that had written that entry.

She imagined his smile, far too clever under arched eyebrows.

Her feeling for him dimmed in an instant. For him to describe what they had shared in terms of such banality. The abuse suffered by Emily for staying, and the abuse she imagined Rita had endured for her departure.

This man had such a hold over how she had defined every aspect of her life — the way she saw herself in every-thing — but the words he wrote to himself were so full of how he loved only him.

She closed the book and continued to stare at herself. Memories of the past tumbled through her mind, and for the first time she could remember, there was no guilt.

Those girls down there, now women on a path that only ended in certain despair, could be helped by the woman she had become. The woman she had been when they were young no longer existed.

That thought took her breath.

And like always, Confidence John was at the center of it.

He was a myth to so many.

She smiled at herself. If only they knew the man in reality. Would they still carry on so? Then she looked down in shame. She had known him, and had carried on so.

She turned and dropped the journal on the edge of the bed. She had bettered herself without him. With the help of another man whom she had aided in turn. She could surely offer the same help for her daughters.

A tap on her door brought her around, and her smile widened as she reached to open it. Jefferson was back. He had given her the time she asked for, but she was all he ever wanted, and she was finally ready to admit that she felt the same.

She pulled the door open, and her smile froze. Rita stood in the hallway with the nun's habit held in front of her. Her mouth twitched. Simone wasn't sure what the movement was hiding. A sneer or a smile?

"May I come in?" Rita asked.

Simone stepped aside and watched Rita pass by to stand with her knees pressed against the edge of the bed.

She glanced over her shoulder. "Will you close the door, please?"

Simone made sure the door latched before she turned

to watch her daughter. Looking at Rita was like studying herself in the mirror. Was this what Jefferson saw?

Rita hesitated, hovering as if unsure whether she should sit on the bed or remain standing.

If Simone got too close, would Rita attack? Did she want revenge? Or did she fear her own mother?

"I don't know what to say to you. What to call you … or …"

"It doesn't matter. I don't know what to call you, either."

Rita shook her head, as if she'd just made her decision. "I'm sorry, but I thought I would be ready for this."

She closed the distance between them, and Simone moved out of instinct to put herself out of reach.

Rita passed and jerked the door open.

"I'll be waiting," Simone said, before her daughter was gone again.

It was almost a relief when the door closed.

Instead of stomping feet going down the hall, there was total silence. As if Rita stood outside the door. Reconsidering?

Simone rushed over and pulled it open, but the hall was empty. Rita had been as silent as a snake.

A *snake* …

Simone gasped and spun around. The journal was gone. Working with the priest? Or stealing from her mother on her own initiative?

How could she?

For a moment she had been standing on the edge of a cliff's edge, and below was forgiveness. It felt like a moment of weakness now, to embrace a daughter she barely knew, a daughter who had every reason to hate her.

She had been so close to freeing herself from the past, only to have the moment stripped away for being so *stupid* as to let that woman steal the journal from right under her nose.

Simone raced to the end of the hall. Her hard heels clumped in sharp echoes in the confines of the back stairs. Though the kitchen was empty, it smelled like cinnamon and baking dough. Claudia was making sweet biscuits. Jefferson's favorite.

She hurried into the parlor to find the four men — no, the *three* men. Her daughter was only dressed as a man. They stood in a loose circle, and she could feel the tension even in the instant of her arrival.

Emily turned to look at her as she skidded to a halt, and even though Simone didn't say a word, Emily smirked as if she knew what would be next on her lips.

Simone couldn't even defend herself against an imaginary accusation.

Chapter Eleven

Emily saw Simone's face and nearly fell to the floor in frustration. Maybe to look up to the sky to shout in a forlorn voice. "What now?"

Jefferson had come in moments before with a bounce in his step, a sly smile as if he held some secret knowledge over her. Buford followed behind him.

She had snatched her hand from Hatken's grip, and he had seemed reluctant to let her go. No longer in contact with him, she suddenly felt uncomfortable with his overtures. Like they were inappropriate. Flirting at a funeral.

She looked away from his wounded gaze, only to see Jefferson's mocking grin, and she stepped back to cross her arms over her chest.

Buford rejoined the group, and the four of them stood in uncomfortable silence. She had just realized they were all three staring at her when Simone burst in with a panting huff.

Jefferson turned, and his arms spread as if he was going to catch her, even though she was several feet away.

Emily met her mother's gaze and was surprised to see

the amount of anger in her eyes. She figured it was only a matter of time before the fight was on.

But Simone surprised her with, "Rita took the journal!"

Jefferson glanced back, including Emily in his confusion. He turned back and spread his hands in a shrug. "What?"

Emily pushed past his shoulder, about to ask Hatken the same thing, but stopped when she saw Father Alonso stagger from the front opening of the church. Blood streamed between the fingers spread over his forehead. "God *damn* it."

Hatken spun to follow her gaze, and when she charged to the door, she wasn't surprised to find him next to her.

Simone whined through an explanation behind her, but the jingling bell above the door drowned out her voice as Emily raced into the street.

The priest held a bloody hand out for support, and she was there to put her shoulder under his arm. Hatken appeared on his other side, and Father Alonso looked at the Indian with an expression of offended sorrow. "*He sido traiconado!*"

Emily put her hand on the priest's chest. "Where is she?"

Father Alonso blinked as he pulled his gaze from Hatken's face. Swung his head around as if watching a bird fly by overhead. He looked at Emily, and some of the fog left his eyes. "*La mujer me traicionó!*"

"I don't know what that means."

Buford came up on Emily's right to take her place under the priest's arm. "He said the woman betrayed him."

Emily pointed to the blood seeping from a swollen egg of flesh in Father Alonso's forehead. "Rita did this?"

"*Sí*. Yes. I escorted her as promised, but she pried the crucifix from the wall and struck me with it. Has she no shame?"

Emily shrugged. "You would be the better judge than me, Father."

Before the priest could respond, Emily turned left and squinted into the distance where the street turned toward the sea. Behind her, Jefferson spoke as if he was in charge. "Where do you think she's gone, Father?"

Emily didn't wait for his answer. She spun around to confront Simone, who shied away as Emily caught her arm. "What was in that journal?"

Jefferson turned from Father Alonso, and his brows drew together. "Take your fucking hands from her."

Simone shook her head, and her eyes fluttered closed. "It was … I don't know. But the last page was about the church in Santa Lucia."

Jefferson dropped a hand on Emily's wrist. "I said to unhand her, sir."

Emily released her mother and turned to face his anger. For now, she would allow his touch to stand. "Are you simple?"

Hatken stood at her shoulder. "She is not a *sir*, Mister Jefferson."

Jefferson looked from Emily to the Indian and back. "I don't rightly care what you are. Touch her again, and you and me are gonna come to it."

"Unwise," Hatken suggested.

"To fight a *woman*? There ain't one alive that can lick me."

Hatken shrugged as his face split in a grin. "If that is what you say, Mister Jefferson."

Simone grabbed the hem of Emily's coat. Like a child trying to get an adult's attention. "Your dowry."

"What?"

"He said it was his daughters' dowries. Buried under the church there."

The fortune she had been seeking. The one that would allow her entry into her father's circle, and pay for his death. Fitting. She had always dreamed that he would purchase his own demise.

She smiled as she turned back around and looked over at Hatken. "I know where she is going."

Hatken looked down the street as she had, and he returned her look with a smile. "It is where I would go."

"Where?" Jefferson asked.

Emily pushed into a run, and she shouted over her shoulder, "To the docks!"

Of course that was where her sister would be going. Over land and through the swamps? Or down the coast and upriver?

The easier route would be by sea.

Hatken matched her speed, and his hair trailed behind him in glossy waves, like the shining wings of a blackbird.

From the quiet businesses around the church to the sales district. Past saloons and port trade businesses. As they traveled from the quiet hum of activity at the edge of St. Augustine to a bustling thoroughfare, they had to slow to avoid wagons and animals, barkers and customers.

They threaded their way through wooden stalls covered in the wares of Seminole crafts and Spanish arti-facts. Steamers from the Atlantic had dumped so many passengers at port, there was almost no room for a man in a hurry.

She thought of pulling her knives, but Hatken's hand on her arm drew her up short. He pointed to the gap between a beer wagon and a whitewashed bandstand. Bouncing up the angled plank to the side of a dark sailing ship was the golden hair of a nun out of her habit.

She looked like a lady pirate returning to command her crew.

Emily threw herself into the press of people moving around the base of a stone statue depicting some Spaniard of local notoriety, ignoring offended shouts and cries. Emily had no time to waste on the fear that her actions might cause unrest.

Perhaps a duel would be entered into, and that would suit her fine.

Rita's ship sat in the gloom of the *Castillo de San Marcos,* staying back as if it was afraid of being touched by the commoners.

At the top of the ramp, Rita turned, and even at this distance, Emily could see her eyes widen. Her sister dropped onto the deck, and only her hair moving along the spaces of the railing gave them a hint as to her progress. Shouted commands from behind them as the ship prepared to make way. The ends of thick ropes arced through the air to free it into the tide.

Emily and Hatken continued their chase to the bottom of the ramp lashed to the dock, but before they could charge to the top, it flexed under the weight of two men lit by the bright sun. Both bigger than Jefferson, they each held a long dagger similar to the machetes carried by farmers through the tobacco fields.

Emily's hands were full of steel, as if the thought itself made the blades appear.

The two sailors descended the ramp with sure steps, their matching smiles an offense to her soul. Smug and expectant. They were between her and her goal. She would not be denied.

She covered the distance in seconds, and as the first

one guarded against her in a movement surprisingly swift for one his size, she moved like a fountain of water into her attack.

A slice through his sweat-stiffened vest brought a freshet of blood from the ribs next to his nipple.

The momentum of his swing continued to bring the machete down, despite his feet halting in shock and pain.

Emily stepped to the outside to vacate the space through which his swing carried his blade. The knife in her right hand came up to slice through his wrist tendons. The knife in her left hand sank into the dirty flesh of his neck, right through a gritty fold under his jaw. Both of her hands were coated in sticky blood.

His machete tumbled to his feet; he jumped to the side as his smug smile melted into terror. She drove her foot into the back of his knee, and he hit the plank like a bale of hay dropped from a thirty-foot barn hook.

The gangway bounced, and for a floating moment, she couldn't feel the wood underfoot. As her toes made fresh contact, she rotated to see the other machete cutting toward Hatken's forehead.

He slipped to the side like he was made of light, out from under the blade in a blink. The thick pirate stumbled by, and Hatken's fist blurred up from his hip to crack off bone.

The sailor's head whipped around as a stream of glistening saliva flowing from his sputtering lips. His knees hit the stone at the end of the plank, and Emily had to give the man credit. He still held the knife.

Hatken danced from foot to foot. He shook his hand as if it was on fire, and his face was contorted into a near-comical wince of agony.

There were shouts and thunder in the street. Shouts

behind her on the ship. It was her sister she still wanted, so she turned back to the sea.

The ship drifted out from under the end of the plank, and there was a weightless heartbeat of horror before the wood — and those standing on it — plunged toward the surf below.

She flung both hands out. Fingers spread wide. The knives tumbled away, spinning spears of reflected sunlight into her eyes.

She hoped the fat sailor would end up beneath her — a human cushion — but she needn't have worried. Her hand slapped stone and her fingers closed on instinct as the ramp fell in a splintering heap below her dangling feet, taking the sailor with it.

Emily kicked the air, struggling to pull herself up. Looked up to see Hatken's strained face. One arm hooked around the stone anchor at the edge of the pier. The other extended to hold her wrist in his fierce grip.

She and Hatken grunted in unison, and she drove her knee down onto the safety of the stone that extended the street to the pier. For a moment, she sat with her head bent forward, resting, and Hatken dropped to sit in the dust next to her. He threw his arm across her shoulders.

Street noise swelled into chaos, and Emily lifted her head to see the glint of Spanish armor. Pikes and swords, and a row of muskets. Distant shouts from the walls of the fort. The grinding of wagon wheels pulled by a team of shod horses.

Jefferson manned the reins, half out of the seat, braced like a buffalo showman, while Father Alonso pulled the open hay cart to a stop in front of the militia line, both hands holding the wooden brake handle. The strain of the pull made the cords in his neck stand out.

Simone swung from the back before it had reached a

complete stop, and her feet churned through the air as she came down.She was across the cobbles in a flash, and Emily rose up to meet her. Grabbed her by the upper arms and pulled her close, lifting the girl to hang in front of her. The pointed toes of her shoes dug into Emily's shins.

She wanted to demand why and how — to finally satisfy the questions she'd swallowed for decades. But the resignation in her mother's face, welcoming of whatever was to come, stopped Emily's mouth. Did she think she deserved what Emily might do to her?

Emily closed her eyes and lowered Simone to the ground. Her shoulders ached with effort, but before she could release her mother, Jefferson bulled in with a growl to grab Emily's wrist.

There were words, but she couldn't hear them. Only the roar of her own rage.

Jefferson threw Simone behind him. Her skirts twirled up like they had coming off the back of the wagon, her tiny shoes like spinning arrowheads. Jefferson barely got a pointing finger above his hip before Emily's knife pressed into the skin beneath his jaw.

She snarled as she drove him a step back toward the wagon, his eyes widen. With surprise or fear? No, he still looked too angry for either. Next time he would know better.

To emphasize her point, she put more pressure on the knife, and he hissed as a trickle of blood colored the edge of the blade. It joined the drying stickiness of the sailor's blood, filling the creases in her skin.

"You touch me again, and I'll lay you open for the crows. *Je ne te laisserai plus jamais.*"

She flung him away, and he staggered into the path Simone had taken. They met in a tangled embrace, and

Emily turned to find Hatken leaning against the stone pillar. His amused smile was back.

The sailor swayed on his feet, and he looked down at the machete he clung to. Looked up at the line of Spanish soldiers. Back to the blade.

He dropped the machete at his feet. Blinked and waved.

Emily sheathed the knife. She didn't want to lose a third one, and when she felt a shift in the air behind her, she readied to defend herself against Jefferson again. But then she turned and saw a young man in tight breeches. Black waistcoat and white lace at wrists and neck. A saber bounced at his side, and he was pulling on the fingers of his left glove.

One of the men she had run into in the plaza? In demand of satisfaction for some slight? Perhaps Emily had run into his lady.

It was no matter to her. She had dueled more times in *jest* than this man had in earnest, of that, she was certain. Before the fop could remove the glove, she drove the webbing between her thumb and forefinger into the flesh above his Adam's apple.

He gagged on lost air, then fell to his knees with a wheezing moan. Emily stepped over him without looking back.

She was prepared to be alone again, but when Hatken joined her at her side, she had to bite back tears of relief.

Reuniting with her family was the hardest thing she had ever done.

Chapter Twelve

SIMONE CLUNG to the edge of the wagon, thankful for even the thin gloves she had managed to grab before Jefferson had flown off like a champion in command of a chariot.

Father Alonso had ascended with some protest, but Buford lifted Simone into the wagon like she was a tuft of dry leaves. She watched him shrink behind them as they charged down the street toward the plaza.

His final wave as he turned to walk back into her school struck her as strangely sad.

Trade had been strong these past weeks, like the final push to sell before the shop closed. So many people moving out, to be replaced by an equal number of strangers. The plaza was full to overflowing.

A line of Spaniards in polished armor burst into the row ahead, and Jefferson veered to hug the faded wood walls of crooked fort structures. Housing and storage, many gone over to rats and lizards. The wagon jounced over the roots of an ancient oak tree. Scraped along the wood of a fish display. The stench of the catch stung her eyes. Ocean-soaked canvas kept the wares cool, but nothing could keep the smell away.

Father Alonso shouted down to the soldiers in frantic Spanish. Spittle flying from his lips. Blood from the wound on his forehead.

Simone rolled to the other side of the cart, and there was an odd motion to the crowd in the center of the plaza, like the ripple of a fish just below the water's surface.

It was Emily and Hatken, a wake of angry shouts and shaken fists behind them. The arrow of their passage pointed to a pier jutting out toward the fort hanging over the inlet.

She narrowed her eyes, and light flashed off a blonde head at the top of a plank moored to a bobbing ship.

She pushed herself closer to the driver's seat and clung to the rough boards. Her *daughters* had caused this chaos. They acted as if something greater was behind them, but she didn't know if it was pushing or chasing them.

They came to a halt so suddenly, it crammed Simone up under the driver's seat. Rough splinters grabbed the cloth of her dress and tore at her hair.

She was out of the tight space and over the side of the wagon in a flash, and it seemed like the ground came at her faster than a horse could run. The impact of her landing jarred up through her knees and hips, and the thought of how much she would hurt tomorrow settled into the back of her mind.

Jefferson often commented on how young she looked, but there was always pain to remind Simone of her age. Worse with every passing month, and she had a feeling this month was going to be a bad one.

She tried to make her own voice heard over the growing cacophony, but she was nothing inside all that noise. The ship was already gone, taking Rita with it.

Emily stood firm next to Hatken, with blood on both arms and scrapes along her jaw. Simone's fear squeezed her heart to a stutter, and she lunged at her daughter, remembering her as the frizzy-haired waif under the stairs whose little voice rose in defiance and anger. Then in pain.

Simone's words became a wail of sound as she reached for her baby. Perhaps she could finally protect her.

Emily drew her into that remembered anger, and Simone welcomed whatever would come. At least she would feel *something* from her. But then Jefferson flung Emily away, and Emily drove *him* back, and her *other* daughter was gone, too.

Simone came to herself with a desperate hold on Jefferson's arm, struggling to maintain her feet as he dragged her back to the wagon.

There was a young man in a black coat sitting cross-legged on the ground, massaging his throat while a pretty blossom of a girl patted his back. By the impressed look on the girl's face, Simone could almost imagine her words.

"Oh, you were so brave!"

She had done the same to Jefferson many times, and it struck her how like praising a dog it was. In shame, she released her grip. No reason to hold him back any longer.

Of course, he didn't let her go. He'd said he never would, and it terrified her that she believed him so. She let him sweep her along until they stood shielded from the crowd at the side of the wagon.

Father Alonso stood in front of the driver's seat like it was an elevated pulpit — shouting orders to the remaining soldiers, crying for peace from the crowd.

Simone noticed how few soldiers there compared to the crowd of ordinary people, and she suddenly felt exposed. "Is this it?"

Jefferson pulled his hand from his neck and looked at his palm with a grimace. "Is this it, what?"

"All the soldiers?"

He nodded and clapped his hand back over a runlet of blood sliding along the side of his throat. "They been cutting out for weeks. Quiet like. Trying to keep it a secret lest these people run riot before Jackson sends his own soldiers down."

She put her hands to her own throat. "My Lord, but that would be a disaster."

"Why do you think I've been so close these past weeks?"

She drew back in surprise. She had seen him as clinging to some puppy-dog notions of love, unwilling to release her from his sight until he got her to submit to his intentions.

Every time she had looked around, he'd been lurking. Or Buford, trying to hide his bulk in a shadow. Or Hatken, moving through a crowd like a silent wind.

She let her hands drop and opened her fingers wide to scrub her palms on her thighs.

Instead of *thinking*, she had convinced herself that she knew with a certainty what was on Jefferson's mind. She was ashamed yet again when she realized she saw only what she wanted, and not what was proven to her. First herself. Then Confidence John. Now Jefferson.

It called into question the very definition of her life. Was she what had happened to her? Was she the memories of what she could no longer control? Was she the product of her reaction to what she experienced?

Jefferson stared down at her as if waiting for her to say something, but she didn't know how to respond to her own thoughts. How could she talk to *him*?

Simone had received revelations before. A moment of

clarity where the pieces fell into place, but the magnitude of this recent thought — that she was fundamentally different from the way she had always seen herself — it staggered her. She reached out for support, and Jefferson's strong hands were there, and for once, holding him didn't feel like an obligation.

Her daughters had come back to her, filled with hate for Simone and for each other. And she'd done nothing to repair that. She knew it would kill her to let them go again, just as she would be crippled if Jefferson was gone.

And yet, she was helpless to fix anything.

She shook her head. "Is this what it feels like to have a family?"

He smiled. "That had been my experience, yes."

She used her free hand to wipe away her tears. "I want it."

"What's that?"

"I want it all. Whatever comes of having a family, I want it. I want you. My daughters. No matter the consequences."

His face creased with sorrow. "Mone, you can't think to make amends with them two."

"I have been unfair to you."

"No," he began, but she urged him to silence with a clenched jaw and a shake of her head.

"I *have*. And I am more sorry than you can imagine. Sorry for you. For Emily and Rita. For myself. But I am no longer sorry for *that man*, for I have you, and I love you, Jefferson Atwell."

"I will do anything for you," he swore. " You name it."

"Help me get my daughters back. *Truly* back to me. If it kills me, I will have my family."

He grinned. "Yes, ma'am."

He took her under his arm with his hand on her shoulder, and they walked back through the plaza like lovers under a full moon. Despite its agitation, the crowd seem to part to let them through.

Jefferson often had that effect, and there was her own reputation as the patron saint of those considered the underclass of the whole town. But she had just realized how few of them were left. Many of her allies were running from a government coming to displace them. Run by a man thirsty for the blood of any brown or red man in his way.

Jefferson had seen it coming and increased his protection of her. Not clinging in fear of unrequited love, but performing a duty made difficult by her unwillingness to see the world around her.

They spoke not a word on the way back home. When they arrived, he held the door open, and Simone realized she wouldn't miss that damn bell. On the heels of that thought was the dawning knowledge that she would be leaving as well. To follow all those escaping the ramifications of statehood, as far south as she could go.

If she could just persuade her new family to go with her.

Hatken and Emily were in the kitchen, hunkered over a sheet of buttered sweet rolls, heads together. Thick as thieves.

Emily played the part of a man well, but around Hatken, her disguise cracked, and the woman beneath showed through.

Not thick as thieves, then, but courtship. How had that happened right under her nose? And so quickly?

Emily and Hatken looked up in tandem, their identical smiles at odds with their rough clothing and apparent injuries. A slick of butter on both pairs of lips.

Jefferson slapped his hat on his thigh. Tossed it like a

platter and it spun to the seat of a stool next to the sink, where Claudia liked to sit at the window while peeling potatoes.

He turned back and spread his arms, and even *Simone* bought into his grin. "You boys leave any for me?"

Emily choked on her most recent bite, and Hatken shook his head.

"Emily is not a *boy*, Mister Jefferson."

It all had the look of a rehearsed routine. How had she missed this as well?

Jefferson grabbed a cinnamon-coated biscuit. He paused before shoving it into his mouth, eyeing Emily with mock disbelief. "Is that so?"

Emily finished chewing. "Afraid so."

Don't be afraid for me," Jefferson said after swallowing the biscuit whole.

That's right," Hatken said. "She's too busy being afraid for *me*."

Emily choked on her next bite, her face turning red as a ripe apple.

Simone felt like she was dreaming. In a moment she would wake, and the misery would settle to bend her shoulders again. In case it *was* a vision, she took the time to look. To see the daughter behind the mask.

And like an oasis emerging to be true, she saw the woman her daughter had become. Not the man she pretended to be, but the person she could have been if not for …

Buford charged into the room with a bottle held out in each hand. "I have the rum."

He skidded to a halt upon finding himself the center of all that scrutiny.

Jefferson wiped his mouth on the edge of a white dish towel. "Well now. What are we drinking to?"

Buford shrugged, but Emily cleared her throat as she grabbed a bottle. She uncorked it with her teeth, and paused before tipping the bottle back for a long pull. "We know where she's going."

Jefferson took the bottle from her and took the second swig. Simone saw Emily's eyes soften. A point for Jefferson.

"Is that right?" he said.

Buford brought the other bottle with him as he settled in next to Simone. "As she already said."

Now all eyes were on Simone. She forced her fingers to relax, to stay quietly in her lap. "I knew before I even read it in the journal. I've always known."

Emily nodded. It was clear she knew as well.

Jefferson passed the bottle to Hatken, who made a careful show of wiping off the rim. "All of that chasing and threatening and blood wasn't needed?"

Emily shrugged.

Jefferson turned to Simone. "So where is it?"

Simone and Emily spoke at the same time. "Santa Lucia."

Emily wouldn't allow her sister to steal her dowry, although Simone doubted she'd use it for its intended purpose.

Jefferson dropped the towel on the wood cart at the edge of the biscuit tray. "And how do we get there? Hire a sailboat? Swim down river? Cut a horse path through the swamp? That big ol' ship the nun left in looks like it's got a keel for speed."

The screen door hinges squealed as Claudia and Yuliana entered, speaking too fast for Simone to follow. When they realized what they had walked into, their faces flushed and Claudia vented a squeal of surprise, losing the hold on one corner of her apron. Potatoes tumbled to the floor.

Simone gave the women a look she hoped was comforting. "*Claudia, donde esta Joshua?*"

In addition to the schooner he sailed along the coast, Joshua — Claudia's husband — also had a ramshackle tobacco steamer he used to navigate through the rivers and open swamps all over the territory. That was how they could get to Santa Lucia.

They might even arrive before Rita did.

Chapter Thirteen

Emily was told that the man's name was Joshua. Even accompanied by his wife and daughter, he did not seem happy to see them. Instead, he grumbled and stomped.

But after a side conversation with Simone — an exchange Emily was certain involved a bag of Spanish coins — Joshua became the spirit of kindness, and within an hour of their meeting, they were on a rattling steamer heading down a murky river toward a small town called Adder.

Everything around this place seemed to be named after things that could kill her.

Since she was already traveling light, there had been very little to transfer aboard — the dank shadows of a crewman's room below the wheelhouse held her belongings with room to spare. Once it was stowed, she emerged into the sunlight, meeting Hatken at the top of the groaning stairs.

A wide deck open on either side for standing passengers. An upper deck for official stations. Rust and rotten wood everywhere. She curled her lip in disgust at the feel of the railing under her palm.

The boat seemed held together by the layers of grime covering every surface. Even the scrolling paint of her name — *Sebina* — was obscured by dirt and soot.

Hatken dropped his hand over hers, and she sighed in frustration. Now she couldn't take her hand off the filthy railing without him thinking she was avoiding his touch.

She clucked her tongue. "You are moving quickly into something you may not want."

"I have already decided. Nothing can change the way of it now."

She looked at him from the corner of her eye, and his smile relaxed her. She looked out at the bank, wondering if they would ever get underway. The churning water hid an untold number of animals just under the surface.

They said the alligators would take a man's leg before pulling him under for the death roll. She suppressed her shudder and returned to the conversation. "Are you implying I have no say in this?"

He held his other hand out with the palm over the water. "It is a part of the flow now."

"What flow?"

"The flow of it all. Everything moving in the current of time."

The boat rocked, as if accepting the weight of a mythic beast. She heard the tumble of coal through the chute above the engine room and looked up at the blue expanse at the edge of the tattered canopy. "You mean destiny?"

"That is a white man's word. There is no word that means the same in my language. A person's life is not meant to be, it is *made* to be."

She smiled. "Ah, I see. You want me because you will it so."

"Yes. Do you not also will it so?"

This was ever a trap, but one she could never resist. "I think I do."

"Then it is part of the flow. You can fight the current to escape where it takes you, or you can surrender to it."

"But what if it takes you to a waterfall?"

He shrugged. "Then you go over."

"Alligators at the bottom?"

He grinned. "It may be."

She slid her hand from under his and turned to face him. "What about what others might say?"

He seemed genuinely confused by her words. "What others?"

"Anybody. A white woman and an Indian man? Or right now, a white *man* and an Indian man making eyes?"

Hatken shrugged. "There is no man that can stand against us."

That statement was full of more conviction than anything she could remember saying. What was it like to just … decide something? This is the way it is now.

Joshua stomped toward them before she could commit.

"You fellas think this thing is gonna start swimming on its own? God *damn*, but that ain't the way of it. Somebody needs to shovel that coal, and you two look fit for the job."

She looked back at Hatken, and they shared an identical shrug before following Joshua back down into the dark, where the heat of the sun was replaced by the angry warmth of a coal fire working the water into steam that drove the big algae-covered paddle wheel.

She and Hatken were shown a shovel each and directed to the pile of fresh coal. They soon fell into the easy rhythm of feeding the flames, and within minutes, her clothes were soaked through.

She had to remain in her undershirt, but Hatken

stripped to the waist, and she found herself watching the light as it played on his skin. White streaks extending past his shoulder. Along his ribs. Scars marred the skin on his forearms, his upper back, his belly. Neat slices and jagged tears. He was a warrior, and his body gave testament to that.

A visit from Claudia coincided with a break, where they drank cool water from a silver dipper and waited for the fire to dim. Pressure dropped as their signal to get back to it, and they resumed their place side by side in front of the burner's iron doors.

There was little conversation amid all that engine noise. Joshua's voice occasionally shouted down the stairs, or he would stomp down to check a gauge or turn a dial.

She bent forward for a spadeful, and the chain slipped out from her collar. The half coin glittered in the orange flames, and she stood with it gripped in her hands so tightly, she thought it would cut right through her palm.

She took a deep breath that burned her nostrils as she stuffed the other half of her father's soul back into her shirt. The she leaned back into the task at hand.

She didn't know what time it was when Jefferson and Buford came down to relieve them. Only that it was dark outside.

She clenched her teeth in a fake smile at the jokes of how *real* men could stoke the fires better than her, and she and Hatken followed the aroma of dinner that seemed to be pulling them up the stairs.

Yuliana served them an incredible meal of chicken and noodles, chased down with warm goat's milk and followed by lime pie.

Claudia approached from the shadows made by the guttering flames of oil lamps hanging from every other post, shaking her head as she gathered the dishes. "Such work makes for dirty men. Mister Emmet. Mister Hatken. There is a bath for you."

Emily groaned with anticipation. A bath would be magnificent.

Yuliana indicated they should follow with a sweep of her arm, and they filed away from the table into the crew compartment darkness, down a long corridor that ended at a door standing ajar. Light from inside barely lit the floor, but Emily's vision was dazzled as she threw open the door, tipping her head back and closing her eyes.

Instead of the oil and smoke caked to every pore, she smelled honey and lavender, the luxuriance caressing her nose.

She opened her eyes and saw two tubs full of steaming bubbles. Hatken closed the door behind her, then threw the bolt.

She should've expected that. Claudia and Yuliana thought her a man, so why wouldn't she bathe in the same room as Hatken? It hadn't occurred to her that her pretense might be harder to keep up in the close quarters of a boat.

Of course, she hadn't expected she'd be shoveling coal in the engine room, either.

Hatken was black from the top of his head to the cotton at his waist. Clean traces of skin from trickling sweat made him look like he was melting. His eyes and teeth shone out like stars.

He bent at the hips as if bowing at court and unlaced his boots. Each one slid off with the sound of dragging air. Then he straightened and untied the sash holding his pants up, and before she could protest, he pulled them down to his ankles.

She turned away in shock as he stepped out of them,

but was betrayed by a full-length mirror in a rusty iron frame that showed her what she'd tried not to see.

Her face was as black as his chest, her arms dark from the rolls of her sleeves to her knuckles. Coal dust coated the insides of her nostrils and formed gritty knives in the corners of her eyes.

Hatken came up behind her slowly, with his hands raised to calm her as he held her gaze in the mirror's reflection. His touch on her shoulder made her catch her breath. Why was she so afraid? It wasn't as if she'd never —

She swallowed and closed her eyes as his hands crept around her arms to the button in the center of her chest. He released it. Moved to the next one. Freed the tails from her breaches. Dragged the suspenders down to hang at her hips.

His fingers crawled along the bandage entwining her body, to the end she kept tucked under in the middle of her back, right at the limit of her reach. He pulled it free, and she lifted her arms as he unbound her breasts.

He let the bandage fall to the floor, and she opened her eyes. He stared at her body in the mirror, and his eyes held no judgement. Just curiosity.

The skin under her clothes was as pale as snow, except for the angry red ridges where the bandage had sat. A shiver rippled down her spine in a violent cascade that chattered her teeth.

With his help, she removed the rest of her clothes, then he stood behind Emily to look over her shoulder, continuing to study her. It was hard not to lift her arms to cover herself under his dispassionate gaze.

She held her eyes to the coin lying against her breastbone until he looked into her eyes again, without accusation or blame. He was just *there*. Like no other man had ever been before. She wasn't sure she deserved such a thing, but refused to let it by.

She turned into him, and his mouth tasted like rock dust and lime.

By the time they were finished, the floor was covered in a sheet of oily water, and both tubs were cold, but the scent of the water was still heaven. Hatken leaned back against the copper side, and she lounged back against him, sitting on his thighs with her feet between his.

He kept trapping her toes under his, and she would escape, only for him to wriggle back on top. A small game that sloshed the water into rhythmic waves.

This would change things, as sex always did. Men expected her to become what they wanted her to be, but Hatken seemed happy with the way she was — even though the scab on his hand from her knife was still red and livid.

She relaxed against him. "This is not a usual thing for me."

"Do you think it is for me?"

She shrugged. "I don't know, for I don't know *you*."

"Even now?"

"You don't know me, either."

"Even now?"

She slapped the water in frustration. "You don't know what's happened to me. Why I'm doing what I'm doing. You don't know what she was like."

He hummed as if thinking of what to say, and she felt him nod his head. "I think we are not what we were."

She looked over to see his face in the angle of the mirror. Thoughtful and serious. "What do you mean?"

"We are not what has happened to us. Instead, I think we are *what we do* about what has happened to us."

"I don't understand."

"Perhaps I don't either." His voice was low and rough with sadness. "A thing can be done. I can hate you. Abuse you. Leave you. Then you live haunted by that thing that action. You are the person that thing has made, not the person *you* have made. Your mother lived that life for a long time before becoming the great lady she is now, and *still* she is haunted by the thing that made her."

He tilted his head back to look up at the ceiling and blew his drying bangs out of his face. "It was her that taught me not to let the thing that was done to me, be the thing that made me."

Could Emily decide the same thing?

It was too difficult to consider. Too much of how she had defined herself was being questioned by a man she had only just met.

Later.

She turned to face him, splashing more water on the floor. He looked at her and the surprise made her laugh. She grabbed a handful of his hair and pulled his head from where it rested on a curl of hammered copper.

She wasn't sure what made her shiver more, the air across her wet back or his kiss.

Chapter Fourteen

Simone pulled the sheet down to expose her shoulder so that the thin film of sweat would cool. She'd been alone all day, and drowsy in her solitude, she sank into her thoughts of the past.

The moment she had convinced Joshua to take them down the Matanzas River had been one of finality. Like the last act of a dying man. Afterward, she had looked in every room of the school and had asked herself what she wanted out of it.

Nothing.

Things collected over a short life born from the ashes of an older one. And neither one was worth carrying forward.

First, she'd just been Simone. Begging for an end while hiding from that ending in terror.

But now she was *Miss* Simone, and there were hundreds of men and women for whom she had been the only kindness. An end to a suffering they hadn't even considered.

But now they were gone. Driven further away by the demons of their country, their family, their choices.

Like the demons she had convinced herself no longer pursued her. The demons she still sought out.

Only occasionally did she consider what it would be like to bring the tincture back to her lips. The bitterness that drove all other flavors away in a muscle-twisting grimace, and then …

Whatever terrible thing she had to do to get the laudanum would be erased from her mind once she had taken it in. The water pipes in the laundry dens weren't the same. Those loosened her teeth and cracked her lips, and the quality of her callers had slipped in response. There was only a certain kind of man who would fuck a toothless whore. And she knew, despite how she might try to convince herself, she would have continued into the dark until she was just another addict wasted away to rags and running sores, waiting for anyone desperate enough to try her.

Always on the edge of destruction. Walking the razor's edge with both hands out for balance, she had never looked down to place her feet. Instead, Simone stared up at the sky and took the next step regardless.

And she had never fallen.

There was an initial pride in her ability to discipline the use of laudanum. Confidence John saw that, and was attracted to her strength. Such a big will for so small a woman. And with him there, she was able to maintain her balance on the blade.

He was murderous excitement. Focused like a glass bringing the sun to a burning point on the ground. He wanted a thing, he chased it, and for years, that thing had been her.

The worst moment of her life was the one when his attention had waned.

The blur of torpor. His rage at finding her inattentive to his desires. He had pulled her from the arms of so many men who would do for her what he wouldn't. Most of those men left in a bloody mess, until the fear of his reprisal was finally worth more than her allure, and she spent many a day alone in withdrawal.

Confidence John had cut her off from everything but what he could offer, and his love turned into a cruelty.

She had tried to convince herself that it was the war. His was a fierce patriotism to an infant nation, and he was legendary on the battlefield.

His energy was divided between her and America. Simone could never be the mistress equal to his nation, so she took a final step. The gold pessary she had used for years to stop conception was placed in a drawer, and Emily was growing in her belly less than a month later.

His anger was violent, and there were many times when Simone thought the baby she had conceived as a trap for the man she was desperate to love could not have survived.

Yet still Simone had stayed on the razor's edge without ever once falling.

Confidence John had long since angered the British, and they wanted vengeance over the loss of a colony, so he left, saying it was for her safety, though it was really to satisfy his spirit.

She fell into a dark depression, and Emily was born already addicted to opium. Pale and thin, she would cry at every moment of the day, only to sleep through the night from exhaustion. The schedule of an addict.

Confidence John heard of his daughter, and returned to see her, but Simone knew he wasn't going to stay. She cried into his shoulder that night in bed, and he murmured apologies into her hair. Still, he was gone the next day.

Two weeks later Simone realized she was pregnant again.

While her figure still allowed, she used her body to provide for a growing family. She resisted the pull of laudanum, and her baby spent most of that first year watching her mother receive abuse at the hands of rough men who saw an opportunity to humiliate someone they could pretend was beneath them.

Simone was clean when Rita was born. She suffered cramping pain for weeks after, and by the time she made it to the mission over the border in Florida, she had a raging fever.

For days she heard Confidence John's voice tell her she was going to die. Her and her babies. *Just step off the edge. Shift your weight and finally let go.*

A bottle of laudanum in her bag, saved for her moment of decision. When she laid the baby in the basket at the front door, she dosed little Rita to keep her silent and calm, then headed down the trade road toward the gulf coast.

The bottle was empty before she reached the ocean, and there she settled into the worst years of her life, somehow failing to punish herself enough, despite her ample effort.

Emily got the worst of it. She grew tall and lanky, and attracted the kind of man that Simone had blinded herself to. The little girl had learned long ago how to be quiet.

They were victims together for a while. United in suffering that had no blame, but that soon passed.

And one day, without warning, Confidence John found her. He looked so fine in the shade of her front door, and all the years spent apart contracted into an instant.

But that was the visit that drove Emily away. One more lie atop all the rest and she was gone.

Simone didn't touch opium after that. Not a single drop. Nor tobacco. Nor alcohol. And it was years before she let another man into her bed.

Across the territory, taking the path of other discarded men and women looking for … if not salvation, then at least purpose.

It was just easier to believe that her babies were dead. In the beach town of Jones Landing, she caught a teenage Creek boy in her cabin. Streaked with white skin as if light filtered down on him through slits in the roof. Bruised and bloody and desperate.

Like taming a wild animal, Simone calmed him with a wordless song she used to hum to Emily. She was surprised to discover he spoke English As if he'd had years of schooling. So she talked to him as if he was a treasured guest in her home, and they spent an afternoon in tentative peace.

They came for him after dark, A group of three dirty Seminole Indians led by a gold-toothed white man. Claimed the boy owed them service. Simone could easily imagine what that service might be, and lied to those men. The first untruth she'd ever told on behalf of someone else.

They looked at her with predatory eyes, but accepted her story that no boy like the one they described was here. The next morning, she and Hatken headed south to the church in St. Augustine. She put her effort and love into him, and her reward was seeing him grow into a good man.

As good as he could be, but what more could be asked of anyone?

No possession was worth more than this opportunity. She would give it all over for even a *chance* to erase her past mistakes. And they were fast approaching the end of a journey that might decide for her, or perhaps even remove the decision altogether.

The bed rocked, and her eyes snapped open. Jefferson slid under the sheet and eased up against her. His stubble sent shivers down her back. She curled away.

"We're ain't gonna be under the steam for the night, just the current. But we should make Adder by morning."

She hummed a single note of understanding and pushed back into him as he settled. He smelled like fresh linens and wood smoke.

He kissed her exposed shoulder and lay with his cheek on her upper arm. "What are we doing?"

She snorted. "I've been asking myself that for hours."

He shook his head, and it made her rock back and forth. "This has been a daisy of a day."

She rolled out from under him, and he propped himself up on his elbow, eyes reflecting the sparkle of moonlight bouncing off the water and in through the window. "How can a thing happen so quickly?"

His sigh blew the smell of whiskey across her face. "It's like it was all perched at the top of a hill, and then somebody kicked it over."

Her mind flashed to an image of her balanced on the edge of a knife. "I don't know what to do."

"This has been coming for months. You *had* to have seen that."

"I don't mean Spain and Florida and Andrew Jackson." Like it was nonsense that could be passed over with nary another thought. "I mean me."

"Don't you always?"

She drew in an offended breath, and then saw his teeth. He was teasing her. "Now, Mister Jefferson Atwell, you behave."

He chuckled. "Now, *Missus* Jefferson Atwell, *you* behave."

Oh yes. The proposal to which she agreed. Another effect of rolling down this hill. She realized how much it had already changed him.

Simone asked the question before she could stop herself. "What makes me worth so much to you?"

His grin disappeared, and his eyebrows drew together. "What would you have me say to that? Good Lord, woman, I care less and less by the minute how you feel about yourself. See it or don't, but I love you."

She sighed. "You are so young."

"Another thing I don't care about."

"I would have wished a man like you for them."

He drew back. "Really? A man like *me*?"

She thought of the haunted wreck he had been when they met. "Well, maybe not *just* like you."

"Don't you understand? I am the man I am *now* because of you. What makes *me* worth it?"

She hoped her answer was the right one. "Me?"

His grin reappeared. "Yes, ma'am."

He lifted his knee to plant between her thighs, , then leaned over and brought his mouth to hers.

He was proof that *somebody* could love her, so perhaps she could learn to love herself.

She hoped her daughters could learn to love her, too.

Chapter Fifteen

EMILY HAD TROUBLE DRESSING. The choice seemed more difficult than usual, but even without her breasts bound beneath her undershirt, and the small sack of rice left out of the pouch between her legs ... she still looked like a man.

A pretty man, perhaps. With the stain fading from her face, the illusion of stubble was breaking. She wore the costume of a lady killer. A cool smile from her would make them swoon.

How lonely she had been since France.

They were the only clothes she had, and Emily had already decided she wasn't *ever* going to wear a dress. She liked the way men looked at her even less when she was dressed as a woman.

The decision wasn't so difficult after all.

Their slow approach required less coal than their acceleration from yesterday, so Buford volunteered to feed the fire until they reached the dock in Adder. He would only have to sit in the dark for a few hours, as she could see the smoke pluming from the town's cook fires already, but it was still a noble gesture, regardless of how small it seemed.

Even Jefferson Atwell, a man she initially judged as a bit slow, seemed genuine in his apology.

Emily knew it was for Simone's sake, and she wasn't sure what made those around that woman want to love her so much. But then, she only had what she knew of her from long ago, and those memories were so colored by hate and loathing ... they didn't fit the expression on Hatken's face when he looked at Simone.

She sighed and grabbed her hat before leaving the room she and Hatken had slept in. Emily was shocked at how quickly she had relinquished her privacy to him.

But as a benefit, the man didn't snore.

The scent of frying bacon beckoned her, and Emily wondered if cooking was all Claudia and Yuliana ever did. She had seen more food at the ready with Simone than anywhere else, except for the colonial army after harvest.

Emily had been around opulence and luxury, but there was a wealth in her mother's life she had trouble understanding. Simone didn't spend it on ease. No fancy forks and knives. No resplendent clothing.

She seemed to spend her money on people. If somebody needed something, she provided it.

The school. The boat. Simone had made it clear she would pay for the horses in Adder, and there seemed to be no end to her riches.

Emily had never seen somebody live so within their means when they could afford so much more.

She leaned against the railing, then immediately drew back in disgust. She turned away to wipe her palms on the thighs of her pants and saw Hatken approach with a steaming plate balanced in each hand.

Biscuits covered in gravy speckled with black pepper,

thick bacon and sliced tomato. He handed a plate over, then turned to look out at the rippling river.

Claudia and Yuliana knew their business, and it was several minutes before she slowed for conversation. "How did you meet my mother?"

His eyes flitted sideways to look at her for a moment before returning his gaze to the water. "She saved my life from the men who would have taken me."

"Taken you for what?" she asked as she scraped the edge of her fork through the remnants of gravy.

"The things such men take children for."

She nodded and licked the fork clean. She had learned to never pass up food on the trail. It was often scarce during times of travel, but it gave her the habit of excess. Sometimes, when the destination had been reached, she continued to feast, only to find her clothes fitting poorly.

"I only ask for perspective. I want no details you are unwilling to share."

His gaze was steadier when he looked at her the second time. "It is a thing I am unafraid to talk about. It is just that I am ..."

He seemed to struggle for the word, so she guessed at it. "Unaccustomed?"

He smiled. "Yes."

He took her plate and stacked it on his, then laid them on the deck at his feet before grabbing a strand of white hair. "I have no tribe. No people. Except those that drove me from every village and town. I had been with a church man for some time, and he did well by me. Taught me to speak. Showed me kindness I didn't know how to return."

He swung her hand as if they were skipping down a hill.

"He was killed by the Gold Son."

"Is that an Indian name?"

"No, but in a way. A man accompanied by three disgraced Creek warriors robbed and burned villages along the coast in Mexico, and the Conquistadors knew of them, and they called him the Gold Son for the set of his teeth. They were all gold."

He stood silent for several minutes, and she allowed him that time. Around the bend of the river, past overhanging brush, was the town of Adder, as sad and brown as she had pictured it. Like almost everything she had seen down here. It was as if the whole town was an abandoned home reopened after a new family moved in.

Spain had taken everything of value on their way out, and the empty land was filled in with blowing sand and brigands ready to take advantage until the new lords came.

Smoke and noise, and the faint aroma of closely-packed man and animal. Sweat and shit, and the smoke of industry. At once repulsive and familiar.

Hatken's grip tightened. "Long after, Miss Simone was there. She could never be a mother to me, but she was much like one, and I always wanted her to suffer less from the things she said she had done. To herself *and* to you."

Emily tried to pull her hand away, but he held tight. She could have fought him, and would have won, but instead, she let him win.

"I'm not used to this," she admitted.

"Unaccustomed?"

She laughed. "That's right. I am unaccustomed."

"I am satisfied with the life I see for me today," he said.

"What about tomorrow?"

"We do not see past what is right now. This day is enough."

"But what about the future?"

He shrugged. "It will always be there. If I look or not."

"But what if you *do* look?"

"You are asking a white man's question."

"I am not a man."

He chuckled. "Then you are asking a white *woman's* question."

"Perhaps, but it is an important one."

He looked into her eyes. Studied them as if he was trying to solve a mystery. "I think you are asking me if I see *you* in my future?"

She nodded before she could stop herself. That was exactly what she had been wondering, and her confusion became suddenly overwhelming. She was not one that ran to hide from *anything*.

Emily now wanted no part of where she found herself — in the uncertainty of purpose and without commitment.

And that was it. She was no longer sure if she wanted to confront Confidence John. Or her mother. Or *anybody* who had wronged her. It seemed such a senseless journey.

She wanted a drink. A *bottle*.

She wanted to have never met this man looking into her eyes with an honesty she hadn't earned.

By the soft sympathy in his eyes, Emily could tell he *accepted* her. What a gift to give another.

Could she do the same thing? Not for him, for it was clear to herself that she accepted him as well. No, could she do the same for others? Could she do it for herself?

"You never answered my question," she said.

He pulled her to him until their foreheads touched. "I hope you will be there, yes."

She didn't recognize herself. In only a handful of days, she had killed four men. Saved a boy from the same fate her mother had saved Hatken from. Reunited with the mother she knew about, and with a sister she did not.

But it was Hatken who made her think twice about killing the man for whom she had started this long journey. The men of her life, real and imagined, seemed to rule her. Perhaps it was time to reclaim the control.

"Look at you two." Jefferson's voice made her start away from Hatken in guilt. Habit perhaps. It bothered her, but Hatken didn't seem to mind. He grinned at Jefferson with Simone on his arm, as if they were courtiers walking to the dance floor.

Jefferson looked from Hatken to Emily, and unexpectedly, his smile was open and kind. "It warms my heart to see young men in love."

Hatken threw his head back and laughed. "Oh, Mister Jefferson, if you only knew better."

"No, I think I'll leave that to you." Jefferson returned his focus to Emily. "So, should we call you Emmet or Emily?"

Emmet was just part of an outfit, but she had worn it for so long, the name nearly sprang to her tongue. It seemed forbidden to claim herself, though. Taking a path less traveled. "Call me Emily, please."

He extended his hand. "Then, Miss Emily, may I say it is nice to meet you?"

"You can say it, though I doubt the truth of it." She took his hand with a laugh, and his grip showed her respect this time.

Then he turned back to Hatken. "We have news, sir."

Simone leaned into Jefferson's arm and nodded. "We are to be married."

Emily's mouth fell open. Jefferson could have been her older brother. Her mother's junior by what? Nearly two decades?

But Hatken threw his arms wide and embraced the pair with love and excitement. A fresh wave of unreality swept through her.

Joy lit her mother's eyes, but Emily also thought she saw a flicker of fear.

She recognized that feeling like it was one of her oldest lovers, and another unexpected feeling bloomed.

Sympathy.

They all leaned to the side as *Sebina* slipped up against the northern dock at the edge of town. The vibration of the contact shivered through the steamer deck like distant cannon fire.

Emily steadied herself against the rocking boat as it settled, and as Simone wiped tears from her eyes, Emily nodded to herself.

Maybe she *could* forgive her mother. Forgiving herself was another matter entirely, but why look to the future?

Today still needed to be lived.

Chapter Sixteen

ADDER WAS A WHOREHOUSE, a schoolhouse, a stripped general store, and a neighborhood of leaning shacks. A last chance for grain and whiskey before traveling deeper into the swamps.

Faded signs warning travelers about the aggression of the "red hatchet" decorated many of the doors off the rickety boardwalk. Despite a lack of traffic, the main avenue was still more mud than road.

Constance Hamilton seemed to run the place: a woman with a laugh that would annoy a coyote and an aroma strong enough to choke a buzzard. But she was willing to sell them a wagon, a broken team of angry mules, three horses, and feed for a week. She had charged extra for tack, and when the deal had been made, Constance had spat in her hand and extended it to seal the exchange.

Simone had refused the handshake, and Constance had shrugged her shoulders like it hadn't mattered, but Simone saw the resentment tighten the skin around the other woman's eyes.

Buford and Jefferson filled the doorway behind her, and the resentment turned back into the obsequious tobacco-stained grin Constance had worn upon their arrival.

Simone couldn't blame her. Through the chance of advancing history, a woman had an opportunity to be her own captain. She saluted Constance, and hoped she could own her future, as all people should. She just wasn't going to touch her.

Simone sat next to Buford in the bouncing seat of the small wagon and angled her parasol against the sun burning into her left shoulder, then made more space between her and Buford to keep from stabbing his back with one of its metal ribs. "My, but it's a hot one."

He grinned. "I hadn't noticed, ma'am."

She directed her attention to Emily. Her daughter sat a horse as well as Jefferson and Hatken, as if she had spent years in the saddle. Another stab to her heart, not to know her own daughter's history. If only Emily would speak to her.

She sighed.

"Why are you so morose, Miss Simone?" Buford's voice was pitched low in a rumbling whisper.

"Thank you, Buford. I just wonder if she will tell me about her life."

"Have you asked?"

"How can I?"

"Just say the words."

"Is it that easy?"

He snapped the reins to keep the mules' attention. "The asking? I think it is. But hearing the answer? That's the hard part."

Emily leaned to the side to reach into her saddlebag, and the horse slowed. Simone watched her daughter lift a waterskin and pull from it. A small trickle escaped her lips and rolled off her chin.

A haunting moment of memory at seeing Confidence John move just as she did, but the moment was broken when Emily turned to catch Simone watching.

Her face was free of expression. Practically frozen. She slid the skin back in the bag and directed her horse to slow further until it fell even with Simone's seat.

Hatken's voice lifted in laughter, and Jefferson leaned over to slap the young Indian on the shoulder.

Simone wanted to be up there sharing their jest, rather than back here waiting for her daughter to tell her how she hated her.

Emily rested both hands on the pommel. Tipped her head to catch the sun flush and extend the shadow of her brim down her arms, hiding all of her face but the grim line of her lips. "Weather on the coast, right?"

Constance had mentioned an overnight storm that seemed to pick up a headwind on its way east, bringing a swell that usually slowed the ships at ocean port. Maybe they would beat Rita to the church. Or intersect at its front door.

"Perhaps it will be to our benefit."

Emily leaned back and nodded. "If not, Rita could still have made the short trip inland to head us off."

Simone didn't know what Emily wanted. To blame her for not arriving in time? Was this some sort of race?

Did lives depend on the end?

They had moved out of Adder as fast as the mules could pull. A slow trot for the horses, but with the thick heat all around and the sticky sand underfoot, progress was what it was. Rita would face the same challenges as anybody else.

"It can't be helped."

Emily nodded. Scanned the horizon. Perhaps she hoped to see the church roof. They couldn't have been more than a few miles away by now.

She swished the ends of the reins at a group of flies crawling in her horse's shoulder. "Have you seen the rails?"

Simone looked into Emily's face, but saw no clue as to what her daughter might say. "No."

"They are a great thing." Emily smiled. "Steel laid on top of thick beams that can withstand the weight of mountains. Held in place with spikes the size of your forearm. Hardy men throwing the hammer down both day and night."

She paused to pull her waterskin back out. "France too, but their system isn't as grand. Just an extension of the rivers, but here? It will shrink the land."

Simone shook her head. This was not the conversation she had expected, but she *had* expected to understand it. "What does that mean?"

"If you can cross the same distance in half the time, it's the same thing as shrinking that distance. A form of magic that happens when you're not even looking."

Simone looked down at her gloved hands. "I suppose."

"What a trick to pull," Emily said. "Imagine a spell that could do that. One that could cut the distance between two people in half."

Simone looked back up to find Emily meeting her gaze. Her daughter smiled. "Imagine that, Miss Simone."

She clucked her tongue, and the horse jumped to match the pace of the other two horses at the lead.

Buford looked up with a broad grin. "What a beautiful day."

"I hadn't noticed," Simone said, nonplussed.

Buford threw his head back and laughed. Birds burst

from the trees at the side of the trail. Shouting back in indignant cries.

Jefferson turned and raised his hand for silence; Buford settled. The three horses spread out, and as they broke through a line of trees, the sand spread out to become the side yard of *Santa Lucia's* clay church.

Jefferson reached behind for his musket and spurred forward to take the lead. Simone was sure it was loaded, but if not, the bayonet protruding from the muzzle looked ready enough.

Hatken removed a pair of flintlock pistols to hold crossed across his lap.

Emily's hand went to her vest, but she held nothing that Simone could see.

The church seemed deserted. Silent and empty. The crumbling walls reached to a tiled roof that seemed recently repaired. Brighter colors in patches along the edges. But still, there was no one around.

No fluttering curtains. No conversation, hushed or otherwise. No smoke. It was as if there had never been anyone here.

She tipped her mouth toward Buford's ear and whispered. "Where are they?"

He bent his neck to indicate the ground beside the wagon. "Footprints."

She followed his gaze, and saw the churned sand depressed into the even divots of a human gait. She couldn't tell if they were coming or going, though.

The front of the church was on the adjacent side to their entry, facing a thin rope of a swampy creek that eventually connected the inlets of the Matanzas to the ocean, with a crooked stone cross sticking up like a broken tooth, its top cracked and jagged on the other side.

A dark doorway met them in the long wall they

approached, and Jefferson slid to the protected side of the horse to throw the reins around a bleached hitch staked into the ground.

Emily and Hatken followed suit.

Feet slapped the sand at the front corner, and everyone turned to face it. Buford steered the wagon to put himself between her and whoever might be rounding the corner.

They needn't have worried. It was a fat priest shuffling forward on sandals. A great bushy beard spread out from his puffy red face. He shook his head and waved his hands as if trying to calm a braying donkey as his teeth peeled back in a wince.

Instead of meeting the three men on the ground, he steered for the wagon. Locked eyes with Simone, and shook his head harder, emphatic with his denial.

He raised one hand and reached with the other, but Buford was there in a flash to intercept him before he could touch her. The priest's eyes widened in terror as his feet backpedaled to no avail.

Despite the man's holy station, Buford carried him the few feet to the wall and slammed the man flat. The wall shuddered, and Simone wouldn't have been surprised to see Buford push him right into the inside of the church.

She jumped down instead of using the steps, and her knees screamed in pain. She hobbled the remaining steps to Buford's side.

Jefferson peered into the dark church. Looked at Hatken with a nod, and the Indian rushed inside with Emily at his back. She must have done the magic trick with her knives, because both hands had filled with steel without Simone seeing it happen.

The priest slapped at Buford's hands, and when the big man let go, he gasped in relief. He turned his eyes to her again and opened his mouth for a large breath.

She heard a rising *zing*, and the priest's head jerked back as if he had been slapped. She saw his brains spread across the adobe wall in a wash of bright scarlet a split second before she heard the report of the shot.

She tasted the metallic tang of his blood, and her gorge rose in a bitter wave to the top of her throat. She heard another *zing*, and wondered who was going to paint the wall this time.

She was lifted from the ground and spun as if in spiraling flight; it wasn't until Simone passed through the doorway that she realized Buford had her under one arm like he was carrying a bag of beans into the kitchen.

Several shots rang out amid shouting. Explosions of disintegrating clay all around her, and she found herself sitting in a heap with her back against the church wall.

Jefferson spun to the window, squinted down the sight of his rifle, and fired in an acrid blast of smoke. Hatken shot both pistols, and in a final moment that shocked her senseless, Rita stepped to another window with her teeth bared and a rifle at her shoulder. She fired and ducked back inside.

Simone shook her head and the room spun like she was back in the flying spiral under Buford's arm. She reached to the side to steady herself, and pain radiated up from her hip. Her skirts glistened with moisture. She took the fabric between her fingers, and they came away red and sticky.

A widening pool spread out from beneath her, and when she looked up to yell Jefferson's name, all she could see was the bright white of the windows. The light swelled to fill her vision, then she saw nothing.

Chapter Seventeen

EMILY FOUND herself standing next to her sister. No longer the nun, Rita was dressed in pale linen, a billowing shirt and breeches, high boots and heavy gloves.

The vision of a pirate.

"Who's shooting?" Hatken shouted.

Emily edged into the window opening. Soldiers at the edge of the trees bent over their guns in frantic activity. The golden plume of a French ground commander bobbed as he charged his musket like churning butter.

Jefferson and Hatken returned fire, and it was just a waiting game to see who reloaded first.

Rita lifted a rifle as long as she was tall, and the window filled with the belch of smoke. The gold-plumed commander spun to the ground with a gout of blood.

She pulled herself back in and slammed her back against the wall between her window and Emily's. She glanced up with a disgusted snarl. "Moreau and the rest of his holdovers."

Without an active volley, the soldiers thought it was safe to close the distance between their location and the church.

Three scurried in a low crouch from dune to dune before taking a position clustered behind the tumbling bricks of a broken well.

It was similar to the one she had seen when first crossing the border. She wondered if this one had a dead priest in it as well.

The soldiers were vulnerable to a good shot, though. As Rita reloaded her rifle, with her rod at the limit of her reach, she shook her head with scoffing laughter. "The French are idiots."

Emily recalled her time among those people to be exciting and productive. She held up a knife point as if striking a mark in the air. "But is Bisset not a French name?"

Rita laughed. "I was raised a Hicks. Technically, I'm Welsh."

The soldiers fired their next volley, and to Emily's surprise, they didn't stagger their fire. She peeked into the front yard, and there they were, ramming fresh shot into their rifles.

A shot from her left brought one soldier down — Jefferson had scored a hit. Hatken fired both pistols, but only a single ball found a target. Emily drew back in to eye him in disbelief. He met her gaze with a shrug.

Emily shook her head, resuming her observation as the third soldier stood to fire. He was completely exposed, and Emily had to agree. Perhaps Rita was right. At least about *these* particular Frenchmen.

Before the soldier could raise his musket to aim, Rita's rifle discharged, accompanied by the bloody impact of her shot hitting the man's throat. His head snapped back, and his musket fell into the open well. His body seemed poised to follow, but he tumbled backwards instead.

Emily scanned the tree line. "Is that all of them?"

Rita shook her head as she reloaded again. "There are two more under the cross."

Emily turned into the dark interior. She needed a moment for her eyes to adjust after staring into the bright of day. "Are you alone?"

"I came with part of my crew, but they're all dead."

"How many?"

"Seven total, two by my hand."

Emily's eyes became acclimated, and she saw the shadow of bodies. Smears of blood on the floor and walls. Snatches of French uniforms.

Then she caught a sight that froze her cold. Simone on her back, with her skirts up. Buford leaned over her like a midwife. Emily closed her eyes and pointed. "What, is she giving birth?"

Jefferson's wordless cry, and his boots sounded off the floor like distant rifle fire. He dropped to his knees and slid the final few feet to his beloved's side.

Buford raised a staying hand. "She is fine! She is fine!"

Jefferson ended with her hand held in both of his. A dazed expression of shock making his entire face hang loose. "Tell me plain, sir."

"She has a furrow along her hip. A lot of blood, but I am staunching it with pressure."

Rita glanced over, then turned back to the window with a sneer and a shake of her head. But it relieved Emily to know Simone was not so bad off as her appearance might suggest.

Hatken rushed by and put his hands over the bandages, and Buford freed himself to move to Simone's head.

Jefferson looked her up and down. "Why is she asleep? Is she dying?"

"I am afraid that was my fault, friend," said Buford.

"What do you mean? Did you shoot her?"

"No, Mister Jefferson. As I carried her into the church to escape the guns, I hit her head on the edge of the door. Not a terrible blow, but I fear I have knocked her unconscious."

"Then wake her up."

Rita snorted, and Emily looked away from Jefferson's comic suffering. "What is it?"

"Why would anybody care about her?"

Emily tilted her head in thought, wondering why *she* cared so much, but the realization that she *did* care was somewhat comforting. It was a relief to know she could feel such a way, for she had thought her emotions for others had been stunted like a diseased tree struggling for the sun.

She tried to ban the image of black thorns from her mind by shaking her head the way a dog might throw water from its fur.

"What are you doing?" Rita asked.

Emily centered her gaze on Rita's face, so similar to Simone's that it was hard not to hate her, despite the fact that she didn't know her. Rita had suffered. Perhaps not as *she* had, but a suffering no less.

If she could resist hating this face, could she resist hating the face in her memories?

She sighed. "I don't know, Rita. Not anymore."

Rita's brows drew together in confusion. "I suddenly find myself with a similar dilemma."

"How did you come to be here?"

Rita glanced back out the window. There were still men out there, but at the moment, Emily only cared about what was *inside* the church. "Why are you alone?"

Rita pulled her gaze from the front yard. "I'll tell you a simple story. The men you killed on the docks?"

Emily nodded, but offered no apology.

Rita didn't seem to expect any. "They were not a part

of my regular crew. I lost four men from dysentery coming down from New Brunswick. Those two were loyalists to Britain, but I couldn't afford to look overlong for replacements. I needed to get underway for a treasure I had heard about in the Florida territory, and like you, I had a key."

Emily remembered the key fitting in the lock of the chest under the Quincy Mission. "Then why didn't you open the lock?"

"My key didn't fit," Rita said. "I left Chase there to see to whoever might follow me, and lo and behold, look who arrived."

"Did he have to kill the priest?"

"Did you have to kill Chase Emmanual? De la Vega?"

Emily nodded with a final certainty. "Yes."

Rita looked away. "Perhaps I can't be as certain, yet you avenged the priest rightly."

"I suppose I did."

"After my rendezvous with the HMS *Stanton*, I was fresh another four crew members, and that was my undoing. They were traitors, you see. Two killed by you in St. Augustine. Two here by my own hand after their betrayal."

Emily turned to see how Simone was doing. Her head was cradled in Jefferson's lap and her eyes were open, looking up into his face. Buford was back at her hip, and Hatken stood to look at Emily with an odd expression of mirth, like he found it all terribly funny.

Emily turned away and looked back out across the sand. A ripple of motion near the base of the cross. An arc of flying dirt and sand. Like a dog digging to bury a bone.

Rita followed her gaze. Cursed under her breath.

"What?" Emily asked.

"They have found it."

She nearly asked what they had found, then remembered why she had come. "The treasure."

Rita held her rifle up. Sighted across the yard. "I was to pay the HMS *Stanton* the contents of Confidence John's chest, but the four crew members hired as replacements were hiding how *deeply* French they were, and they had set up this little ambush for me. Five crewmen murdered by French soldiers."

"And another dead priest," Emily said. "We will be well-known in hell."

Rita snorted laughter. "As long as I am joined there by those that deserve it far more."

Emily knew who she was talking about. She had shared the same sentiment for so long, it was odd to no longer feel it. "What is the HMS *Stanton*, and what were you paying it for?"

"A renegade warship. Protection for an honest seafaring vessel like mine."

"You just want their guns at your stern?"

Rita smiled and gave her a wink. "The open sea is rough on a woman alone. Especially one as fair as I. Perhaps I'll use their guns as an assurance to land on *El Halconito*. Pay our father a final visit."

Simple revenge. "But you were betrayed by the French crewman you hired, and now here we sit, sisters united in an effort to retrieve our heritage. And you would have kept it from me, Dear Sister?"

Rita pulled her rifle back inside the window. "What would you have done? Surely, the same?"

"As I said earlier, I don't know what I'm doing anymore. I intended to use the treasure to enter our father's tournament."

"And then?" Rita whispered.

"His death at *my* hands."

Out of her periphery, she saw more movement across the yard. Two French soldiers struggling into view. Another pair popped up to cover the first two with a rifle aimed at the church. Each with a second rifle on a sling.

Emily leaned back into cover. "I thought you said there were only *three* more."

"I wasn't wrong. There are certainly three men out there."

Emily turned to the people that had become her new family.

"Hatken," she shouted. "You and Jefferson arm yourselves and get your asses over here!"

She didn't wait to see if they complied, but Simone was leaning on one elbow, so it looked like she wasn't going to die. At least, not just yet. Hatken trotted up to her side with his pistols. Jefferson followed with his rifle on his shoulder, but he looked back at Simone the whole way.

As they settled, she glanced back through the window. Two soldiers struggled to stand with a dark chest held between them. The other soldiers closed in front of them with their rifles on the church. They started a scuttle that would lead them into the trees several yards behind them.

"Damn them!" Rita shouted.

Emily grabbed her sister's shoulder. "Give Hatken your rifle."

Rita pulled herself away from Emily's touch. "I'll not give that savage a *thing* of mine."

"Fine, then give it to Jefferson. He's fine and white, *and* he's going to marry our mother."

She turned to Jefferson and grabbed his lapels. His eyes focused on hers. "You fire on them so they fire back. You have lead shot to match them, and I suspect Rita and I can cross that distance before they can reload all four." She turned back to Rita. Held her knives up in front of her face. "Do you see?"

Rita narrowed her eyes, but she nodded. "Are you capable?"

Hatken laughed. "She has no equal I have seen."

Rita looked up at him. "I don't know you."

"But I know you," Hatken replied, "and more importantly I know *her*."

Rita clenched her jaw. Held her rifle out with a stiff arm. When Hatken grabbed it, she let go without a word.

Emily spun away. Rita's steps echoed her own, and when they met at the side door with the dead priest's shoes sticking into their path, Emily paused and looked behind her.

Jefferson and Hatken waited with their backs against the wall. Emily nodded, and they all burst into motion. She and Rita rushed to the side of the wagon, then jumped low into the open.

Both sides fired in near unison. Explosive echoes slapped her eardrums with vertigo, and a puff of dust erupted an arm's length from her feet.

She only counted seven shots.

She rose to her full height and drove her legs into a sprint. Only one soldier held the chest. The second was on his seat, holding a bloom of red against his chest.

Only seven shots because one of the riflemen lay on his back with his feet splayed. The other rifleman bent to his rod in a frantic attempt to reload before she got there.

His frantic look slung sweat from the hair plastered against his forehead. She crested the dune with her knives at the ready, and he spun the rifle around to threaten with his bayonet.

The soldier fighting to move the chest dropped the weight and drew his sword out of its scabbard, standing over the chest like it was his slain comrade.

The rifleman charged with a wild scream, and he drove

his bayonet at her with the precision of a movement drilled into him over many years. As Jefferson had slid to Simone's side, so did Emily slide under the man's thrust.

Heat bit into her knees, and the air of the man's strike passed overhead. She drove her blade to the hilt into the inside of his leading thigh with her left hand as the right circled around to sink inside the flesh of his lower back just above his belt.

He spun away from her impact, and she rotated the opposite way to find her feet. His scream of aggression became a shriek of agony, and she swept his clumsy swing to the outside. His leg gave out under him, and his arms widened like a promised embrace.

A slice across his throat completed her turn, and she heard him fall behind her as she jumped to engage with the man guarding her treasure.

He recognized her skill with the blade, but he was still not prepared for a master. She strapped his initial strike on the crossguard of her knives. He was fatigued from digging, from heaving the chest from the dirt. His strike had nothing behind it.

She pushed his blade across his body to expose his side, and drove a knee into his ribs. He wheezed like a shredded bellows and staggered back. His fingers loosened, and his blade dipped.

She swatted it on the flat, and his saber rolled over his grip. She let a knife drop to bury its point into the dirt as she grabbed the saber by the handle a moment before it hit the ground. Down to one torn knee where she spun as he tried to jump away.

The tip of his own blade whipped up to bite through flesh and bone under his jaw. He died on his back staring up at the bright sky, drowning in his own blood.

Emily dropped the saber onto the man's quivering

chest, then turned to find Rita standing bent over, hands on her thighs. Her sister shook her head between gasping pants. "That was not fair."

Emily looked from Rita to the dead men at their feet. "Not fair for whom?"

Rita tipped her head back and took a deep breath. "So fast."

Emily lifted a shoulder in a shrug and turned to the chest, squatting in front of it. She had hung the coin around her neck, but still carried the key in her watch pocket. She fished it out and fitted it in the rusty lock.

Rita bumped her to the side as she dropped down to watch. Emily glanced over into her excited eyes. They each drew a breath, and Emily turned the key.

It held fast.

She tried again, but still it wouldn't move the lock.

Rita gasped. "That's why my key wouldn't fit the other one."

When Rita pulled out a similar key, she suddenly understood. Her key for the chest in Quincy. Her sister's for this one.

Emily withdrew her key and sat back, allowing Rita to take her place. She turned *her* key, and the lock clicked open. Emily pressed her shoulder into Rita's and they lifted the lid together.

Chapter Eighteen

SIMONE RESTED her head back against the cool wall while
Hatken held a damp cloth to her forehead. Her hip was a
burning fire, and her head thumped with her heartbeat.
She opened her eyes, and saw only the blurriest light.

"You will be fine, Miss Simone," he said.

But Simone didn't believe him. She could smell blood.
So much of it. Her throat tightened against the bile that
burned there.

A moan of pain right next to her, and she had to resist
asking who it was. She had already been told it was a
wounded stranger. Dead, save for the final muttering of
prayers.

Old wooden pews had been turned over and stacked
against the far side door, propped into a line of cover in
front of the windows. Evidence of activity before their
arrival.

She pulled Hatken's arm away. "Where is Jefferson?"

"He is coming, Miss Simone."

She didn't believe him. Jefferson was dead, and Hatken

was saving her the pain. She shook her head. "Help me up."

"I don't think that wise."

She pushed him away and drew her legs up under her with a hiss of pain. He rested his hands on her shoulders, and instead of holding her down, he helped her stand.

He supported her until she got her balance centered on her belly and settled into the new elevation. After a few breaths, she seemed better. She cracked her lids open, and everything seemed less bright. The thump in her head dulled to an ache, from a gallop to a trot.

She looked around at the mess strewn across the floor. "What happened here, Hatken?"

He stepped back with a shrug. "A gunfight."

"Over what?"

He shrugged again. "We will soon see."

With that, there was a scrape across the doorway threshold where they had tied the horses. Grunts and footsteps, and Jefferson's wide back blocked the light as he backed into the church.

Buford followed, and between them they carried an old chest. Pirate's treasure.

She held her breath, resisting the urge to fly to him until he had lowered the chest to the floor. When he stood back up with a stretch, she lunged at him in a crooked run, hitting him broadside and wrapping her arms around his chest. He staggered back, then curled over her with his mouth pressed against the crown of her head. She sobbed, unsure if he could even hear her words. "I thought you were dead."

"Oh, Mone. I thought the same as you."

"I can't go on," she said. "I can't watch you die, and Emily is intent on more death ... I can't."

He pulled her to arm's length. "They had a similar head."

She wiped her tears and winced as a fresh wave of pain spread across her forehead. There was a lump over her temple that felt like a boulder. "Who?"

"Your daughters."

As if summoned, they entered, like a past image of Confidence John and Simone. They carried the body of a soldier hung across their shoulders by his outstretched arms — they turned as one and dropped him to groan at the base of the wall.

She watched Emily squat in front of the soldier. She grabbed his coat at the shoulders and heaved him upright. Drove him back into the wall.

The man's face twisted with pain. His voice was torn and hoarse. "*Il n'y avait plus*."

Emily shook her head. Simone looked up at Jefferson. "What did he say?"

Jefferson shrugged, but Buford leaned toward her. "He says there is no more."

"No more what?"

Emily slapped the man on the cheek. His head rolled to the side, and his eyes sprung open to look at her with hatred. "*Je le jure*."

"He swears," Buford translated.

A knife appeared in Emily's hand, and the French soldier froze. She leaned forward to press the steel beneath his left eye. He stared over the blade with terror. He opened his mouth, and a spill of words tumbled out.

Simone turned to limp away, and Jefferson supported her with his strong arms until she found a pew still sitting upright. She lowered herself with a groan, and he dropped next to her.

She felt so much love for him. So much love for her

daughters. Had she truly paid for her mistakes, to deserve such a reward?

She burst out laughing at the thought. Jefferson jerked away as if he had been shot and made her laugh harder. Surrounded by the dead, she sat with a bullet wound in her hip, and a dizzying lump on her head. If this was reward, she might ask for the punishment next time.

She sobered to find Emily and Rita standing in front of her. Light from the front windows surrounded them with a burning aura, and she couldn't see their faces, but she felt the mood shift.

She knew what bad news looked like.

She resigned herself for the punishment she had just asked for. "What did he say?"

Emily took a slow breath. "He said he and his men were in league with the British."

Jefferson growled. "What British? The *nation*?"

Emily held up her hand and shook her head. "No, they are part of a rogue unit called *Fer Et Feu.*"

"Iron and Fire," Buford translated.

Simone's smile felt strained. "Thank you, Buford."

Emily pursed her lips in agitation, and Simone ducked her head. "Apologies. Please, continue."

Emily shared a glance with Rita. A look that seemed to share years of history instead of days of antagonism. Emily looked back to Simone, as if she was reporting to a superior. "Yes. *Fer Et Feu* is a group of soldiers who want the war between America and Great Britain to continue."

"But it *does* continue," Jefferson said.

Emily shook her head. "Not like this. Rita's crew told this French unit of Confidence John's treasure. A legend in some circles, like the ones in which we often found ourselves, but we had the advantage of inside information.

Until her crew was infiltrated by these men, in a secret pact with the HMS *Stanton*—"

Jefferson was on his feet so quickly, it was as if his wake pulled Simone into the space he had just occupied. She threw down her hands to keep from tumbling from her seat.

Jefferson pointed a shaking finger at the French soldier sitting on the floor. "They are in league with those butchers?"

"So he said. And he laid his plans bare."

Jefferson took a step and jutted his chin forward. Simone could see his rising anger, the temper she had tried so hard to help him tame. "Tell me," he demanded.

Emily's eyes softened with sympathy, and Simone couldn't figure out why.

" "The money would pay the captain of the HMS *Stanton*, and the warship would steam to *El Halconito*, where its guns would rend the island asunder."

"But Spain is withdrawing from the territory," Buford objected. "They surrender ownership of that island, just as they do Florida."

Jefferson dropped his hands to his side as if accepting defeat. "Who will control the island after they leave?"

"Florida as a *state*?" Buford asked.

Emily nodded. "*El Halconito* is becoming a part of the United States of America."

Simone gasped, clutching at her throat with both hands. "But that would be an act of war."

"Commander Moreau said as much. The HMS *Stanton* is prepared to burn on the ocean. They will happily claim the attack in the king's name, and the revolution will be but an echo compared to what will come."

"Ah," Buford said with dawning understanding. "And

the French will move in with their native allies. Regain territories and vengeance."

Rita shook her head. "I don't believe it is the stance of Paris to re-wage war on America as a whole. I believe it akin to mischief-making."

Simone looked up in horror. "*Mischief?* At such a level."

Rita shrugged. "There are some who define their words with a different dictionary than you, Mother."

Simone fell back in shock. Rita had called her *Mother* without weight or bitterness. Her reaction seemed unnoticed, so she drew herself upright and squared her shoulders. "What can we do?"

Rita laughed. "To stop it? Against the guns of the *Stanton?* Nothing. Besides, we don't even know if they will do it, now that there is no payment."

Jefferson covered his face. "You don't understand. I used the word *butcher*, and it fails to describe the crew of the HMS *Stanton*. They are *embittered* by the outcome of our revolution. Living as pirates in the waters around Cuba. Pestering trade and hounding the efforts of America *and* Britain to defend the seas. It is not the money they want, it is the opportunity."

Instead of asking how he knew what the *Stanton* wanted, Simone raised her hand for attention. "Then the question remains unanswered. What do we *do?*"

"We may not be able to stop them, but we can bear witness," Hatken said.

Rita cut the air with the edge of her open hand. "We aren't sure they're even going to do it."

Emily pointed at Moreau. "He said the *Stanton* was hiding in a cove less than twenty miles south of *El Halconito*. I think they plan to do it regardless of payment. In fact they may be more likely to do so if payment is withheld."

"Spiteful," Buford said.

Rita spat. "Just like the French."

Simone saw Emily's forehead wrinkle in anger, but there wasn't time to ask why. She pushed to her feet and pointed at Rita. "The ship you escaped on. I assume it's yours?"

Rita drew herself up with pride. "All mine, pitch and pale. I call her the *Falcon*."

The silence stretched out, and Rita's face fell into confusion. "What?"

Simone shook her head. "How soon can we be out to sea?"

"We're anchored in an inlet a mile east. We just came in under a storm, so there is need for repairs, but my crew is down by several hands. We could not fend off attack or boarding. But I am known in these waters, and you look like hard men. Especially my sister."

Hatken's laugh bounced off the high ceiling, and Simone hid her own smile behind a gloved hand.

Emily crossed her arms over her chest. "Moreau died before he could tell us the day they had agreed upon, but I believe Andrew Jackson is on his way down here as we speak. It wouldn't surprise me if it was this very day."

Simone inclined her head toward toward "And what of that?"

"I told them to leave it in the dirt of the yard."

"But you never said why," Jefferson protested.

Emily walked over and kicked the lid open. There was naught inside but rocks.

Chapter Nineteen

EMILY MISSED Claudia and Yuliana's skill — on the Falcon, there was nothing to eat but hard cheese and harder bread, washed down with water that tasted like gunpowder and salt.

She had taken the time to wash the sweat from her face, sluicing the drying blood from her hands and forearms. What she had been, what she was, and what she was becoming were no longer a solid notion. They all flowed together with her new understanding of what life truly was.

She had always been aware of war, but not from a larger perspective than her own selfish growth. She had often thought a duel was warfare. And she had seen enough horror from the blade to convince herself it was so, but the hollow look on Jefferson's face as he sat on his horse with nothing but the thoughts of the revolution made her believe otherwise.

They were all deferring to Simone. She had even turned her *own* will over to the woman, as if in silent agreement that she commanded them. Even Rita had settled under their mother's hand.

For the tenth time, Emily slowed her horse to keep pace with the mules pulling the wagon. Stubborn animals, they wouldn't move above a fast walk no matter how many times they heard the reins snap.

The sun lowered behind them, and their shadows stretched out before them like rippling carpets. By the time they were at sea, night would be upon them.

She sighed and looked off to the side of the trail, into the thick layer of overgrowth. She imagined a horde of French soldiers coming for revenge against her.

There was a time when the thought would not have entered her mind. She was as sure in her right to live whatever life she chose as she was in the knowledge of her past. But now both of those things were on loose ground. Finding herself with unsure footing was no way to begin a fight.

She glanced back over her shoulder. Simone sat next to Buford, with Rita astride a bag of mule feed. Jefferson watched the ground pass beneath him. Hatken braided his horse's mane.

Hatken said he wouldn't look to the future, for today was enough to worry about. How to be so free? To look back at the things that had happened to him, to remember the horrors committed to his mind and body, but not think of a day when he would be free of it?

And perhaps that was it. Why wait to be free?

Choose freedom for today.

The trail split in the distance ahead. It curved to the right where the dense growth surrendered to a view of the ocean. The left-hand path rose to climb a gentle hill. Through the swaying leaves, Emily saw the shadow of the *Falcon*'s mast rocking back and forth.

Rita directed them to the left, but as the mules felt the weight increase on the elevation, they stopped, dropping their heads and refusing to continue.

Emily slid from the saddle, turned to pulled her pack free, and loosened the straps so the leather burden slid from the animal's back. It shied away from the noise with an offended *whuff* through its nose, and Emily stepped in to relieve the halter.

Jefferson and Hatken followed suit. They dropped all the gear they didn't need right at their feet. Buford dismounted the wagon with a grunt as his feet hit the sandy earth. He unhitched the mules, and even though they were free, they kept standing like statues.

Obstinate animals.

With their personal belongings on their backs, including a small bag hanging over Simone's right shoulder, they took the rise the mules had refused, and as the setting sun scorched the sky with fire, they stepped into a clearing at the top of the bluff.

A lantern burned next to a wooden plank lashed to the port side of the *Falcon*. Rita took the lead, looking back at Simone as she passed. "We can go out with the tide, so we won't need any men on the oars."

Simone nodded, but Emily doubted that it made any more sense to her mother than it had for *her*.

The slight rise of the path had put them even with the deck. Just a handful of feet above the water. Standing broad to it made the ship seem much smaller than when it had pulled away from St. Augustine. The failing light made it seem even smaller still.

"Who goes there?" shouted a voice from the shadows.

Rita shouted, "Just a fair-haired lass with a love of the sea."

A thick man stepped into the feeble lantern light, and a

golden glint reflected off the muzzle of his musket. Heavy with muscles, and with hair as dark as Hatken's. His bare feet were silent on the deck. He tipped his head to see down the length of the barrel. "Captain Rita, I wonder?"

She bounced down the plank like it was a practiced dance. "Wonder no more, for it is I."

Without sparing a look at the rest of them, he leaned the gun at his side and threw his arms wide. She ran into him with enough force to make him grunt, and they exchanged a kiss with more passion than was strictly proper in mixed company.

Rita pulled back and turned to look back. "This is my first mate, Mister Ambers."

"I am her *only* mate."

Jefferson nodded his approval, and Emily couldn't help laughing.

Ambers turned back to look down at Rita's face with concern. "Where is Johnny and them?"

She shook her head. "We were betrayed."

"Like hell. Those French bastards?"

She nodded, and he stomped both feet before spinning with his fists in the air. "I *knew* it."

Then he paused. Looked over his shoulder as the rest of her group came aboard. He dropped his hands and faced them. "So who is this lot?"

Rita shrugged. "My family."

And just like that, it was so.

Ambers looked up at the sky and spread his hands as if beseeching a higher power for help. Emily could almost make out the words of his silent prayer. *This woman.*

Emily hid her smile as she approached. "Are we leaving soon?"

Rita leaned back against a roll of thick rope and crossed her arms. "With what crew?"

"How many are left?" Emily asked.

Ambers held his hand up to tick off fingers. "Me, Smith, Claw, and the captain. I never much cared for them others, anyway."

"Still, there were five men in my company who knew what they were doing under the sail," Rita said. "Shall we just teach you how to crew a ship in their stead? In the dark?"

Emily reached up for comfort from the knife under her vest. "In the morning, then?"

"That *must* be the plan." Rita pointed in the direction they had come. "Will you pull in the gangway and replace the railing, Mister Ambers?"

Ambers turned to the group. "Should I take orders from a woman?"

His grin made it clear he was joking. Probably a common joke between them. Maybe for years.

Hatken seemed to take it seriously. He nodded his head as if accepting some hard-fought wisdom. "*This* woman? Yes."

Ambers laughed. "I like this one." He clapped Hatken on the shoulder as he passed. "Come help me, friend. You'll be crew, yet."

Rita spun to open a small door. Flickering light spilled across the deck, and when she closed the door behind her, Emily had the shape of that illumination still in front of her eyes.

She blinked and shook her head. Turned to lean on the railing. Looked down at the stars reflecting off the water.

There was no one for her. Buford was his own man. Jefferson and Simone stood at another section of railing. Hatken was learning a new skill. She didn't want to be alone with her thoughts — emotions sickening in their familiarity, and now she was lost as to how she might channel them. Lost without her pledge to herself. Her long-made promise to get Confidence John back for all he had done.

And it was no longer for what he had done to her, but what he had done to Simone and Rita. How could *her* tide turn so suddenly?

The small door opened back up, and Rita stepped out of the spread of light, followed by two men dressed as nautical twins, some foreign uniform with which Emily was unfamiliar. Their whispered conversation confirmed it — a language she could only guess at — and she dismissed them as they passed without a single glance her way.

Rita approached, pulled her hair back into a fresh tail. "Smith and Claw will weigh anchor," she said. "Then we will cast off into the current which already tries to push us out to sea. I must man the rudder, but when we are beyond the beaches of this inlet … perhaps we can speak."

Emily could only nod. The way emotions had been bursting from her lately, she trusted neither her thoughts nor her words.

"We may even be able to see the lights of *El Halconito* when we emerge from the bluffs."

Rita looked into Emily's eyes as if waiting for something, but Emily was at a loss for a reply. Nothing seemed to fit the situation, as she had never been in one quite like this.

There was a flash behind her, as if a star swelled while falling into the sea. An echo of an explosion rolled across the water like an approaching thunderstorm.

She spun in time to see the horizon erupt into a red curtain of fire. Another tumbling roar, and then the sky exploded into light and sound.

"Is that fireworks?" Emily asked. "Is the tournament underway?"

Rita shook her head. "I saw the Chinese freighters debarking from Cuba a week ago. Maybe they have delivered their cargo?"

"Bombs," Jefferson said.

Emily turned to find him staring at the glow in the distance with empty eyes that gleamed with unshed tears. She grabbed his arm. "We are too late?"

He turned his gaze on her, and it was as if she could see to his depths. He shrugged before turning back to the fire in the sky. "Is it ever so?"

Was that the HMS *Stanton* destroying *El Halconito*? Was that the British warship killing her father? Starting another war?

"What would we have said had we gone?" Emily asked no one and everyone. "Dear Father, it is I, and I am here to kill you, you son of a *bitch*!"

She ran toward the explosions, and they blurred into a million red sparks as her eyes filled with tears. "Damn you! You have made me just like you! I *hate* you! You have torn everything good and pure from my heart and left only a festering darkness!"

Her knees buckled, and she tumbled down to the deck. She leaned forward and pressed her head to the wood. The coin tumbled out in a chiming jumble. She grabbed it and yanked it down, but the chain didn't break.

She screamed in frustration and pulled again. Three pulls later it finally came free, and she looked at it in her hand. A broken coin. As they all were.

Broken.

Robbed of her ending, Emily's story would instead decline into war. It felt like punishment. God had damned her for the sin of thought. It didn't matter the awful things she had done on her quest. The initial glimmer of revenge had set her against the Almighty, and this was how she would pay.

Hesitant footsteps at her side, and Emily prayed it wasn't Hatken. She couldn't handle his gentle forgiveness. Not now while she still smelled of regret and despair.

The faint shadow from the lantern behind them revealed the shape of Rita. The first person to offer comfort was her sister. It twisted her heart that she couldn't be as accepting.

Rita stopped at her side and dropped to her knees. She looked at Emily's hand in shock. "Where did you get that?"

Chapter Twenty

SIMONE WOULDN'T BE CONCERNED for that man's life. She refused to shed a single tear.

Instead, she would pour her soul into the man at her side, and the daughter screaming her pain at the phantom in the distance. Emily's tortured voice was a spike into Simone's heart.

No, she wouldn't waste a *thing* for Confidence John. She had only so much to give, and there were more important people than *him*. People who asked for nothing in return.

Like Jefferson, who had not demanded her love, but had waited patiently for it. Like Hatken and Buford. Claudia and Yuliana. Even Joshua, in his gruff way. The hundreds of families she had reunited. The men and women she had shuttled to safety.

In this tragedy, Simone could finally see what her life had become. Just as Emily had cried out for a life lost, she had felt her heart swell in understanding.

Simone could be a better person. A *good* person. And

for the first time in her life, she dared to believe that perhaps she *was* one already.

She moved toward her daughters, pulling Jefferson along with her. Hatken overtook them to stand at Emily's back. He reached a hesitant hand toward her shoulder, but as another wrenching sob tore from her throat, he pulled his hand back and looked at Simone in panic.

She had to agree. She didn't know what to do, either.

Rita rocked at her sister's side. Then she dropped to the deck to land on her knees as if her leg bones had turned to water. She stared at Emily's hand.

"Where did you get that?"

Simone got close enough to see over Emily's shoulder. She held a piece of metal, like a coin bitten in half. Simone had never seen it before.

Emily's head rose as if she struggled against a weight, and her lips curled into a sneer. "My *father* gave it to me." She dropped her gaze back to her palm. "He told me it was the other half of his soul."

Rita's trembling fingers rose to her throat, and she pulled a chain from the neck of her shirt. "He said to keep it safe."

Emily jerked her head up in surprise, and another sob escaped through her clenched teeth.

In Rita's hand was the mate to the half-coin. As Emily's sobs gained strength, Rita reached the coin out until they were suspended side by side. It was a perfect fit.

Rita leaned over and threw her arm around her older sister's shoulders, and together they sobbed.

Simone looked up to the ripple of red light fading into a deep orange. She envisioned the entire island in flames, but felt no satisfaction. Only an increasing sadness.

Confidence John had known about Rita. He had

known about everything. She and her daughters could spend the night mourning for all they had lost, and it wouldn't matter.

They would never be free of Confidence John.

A young woman with a little girl's dream. Two handsome suitors. And an adversary determined to crush her before she stands a chance.

Lily Whistler has a dream, birthed from the fanciful Parisian memories of her late mother: to open a floral shop called La Fleur de Blanc, selling only white flowers.

Get La Fleur de Blanc today!

A Quick Favor...

If you enjoyed this book, please take a moment to write a short review on your favorite online bookstore so other readers can enjoy it, too.

Thanks so much!
Harmony Reed

About the Author

Harmony Reed writes revelatory stories about what it means to live, how we can become more fully human, and how we can shed the lies we've been living by and embrace our truth. Her fiction melds the large-scale with the deeply-personal, yielding insight into the human psyche and the world we all must move through. If you enjoy authors like Michael Chabon and Jodi Picoult, movies like *Big Fish* and *Little Miss Sunshine*, or shows like *Orange is the New Black* and *This is Us*, you'll love Harmony Reed.

Spitting Image

Drink

La Fleur de Blanc

Confidence John